Sod Schoolhouse

Courtner King
Bonnie Bess Worline

CAPPER PRESS
Topeka, Kansas

———————◆———————

Published by Capper Press
1503 SW 42nd, Topeka, Kansas 66609

Editor: Samantha Adams
Assistant to the Editor: Pat Thompson
Cover Illustration: Bruce Bealmear

ISBN 0-941678-55-5
First printing, May 1996
Printed and bound in the United States of America

———————◆———————

For more information about Capper Press titles,
or to place an order, please call:
(Toll-free) 1-800-678-5779

Capper Fireside Library

***F*eaturing**
the most popular novels previously
published in *Capper's* magazine, as well as
original novels by favorite *Capper's* authors, the
Capper Fireside Library presents the best of fiction in
quality softcover editions for the family library. Born out of
the great popularity of *Capper's* serialized fiction, this
series is for readers of all ages who love a good
story. So curl up in a comfortable chair,
flip the page, and let the storyteller
whisk you away into the world
of this novel from the
*Capper Fireside
Library.*

*To all those family members
and friends who lived these stories
before we wrote them down.*

*Courtner and Bonnie Bess
Brawley, California, 1996*

Contents

Sod Schoolhouse

Ad Astra Per Aspera
"To the Stars Through Difficulty"
(Kansas' state motto)

PREFACE

W<small>HEN THE</small> U<small>NITED</small> States bought the large area of land called "Louisiana" from France and opened it for settlement, people from all of Europe poured in. Some were well educated and were from rich families; many came to promote freedom and democracy. Other settlers were merely poor peasants who sacrificed a great deal to reach a place where their children could own land and be educated. Poor people from the South also joined the settlers in the newly available territory.

Western settlers were often adventurous regardless of their origins. They explored new land and new ideas such as freedom for all people and citizenship for everyone, including Negroes and women. After the Civil War Negro males were given the right to vote, but not women. Kansas, among other states, carried on the suffrage crusade. Kansas gave women the right to vote in elections for school board members, shocking many Easterners.

Settlers in the middle and far West also supported a woman's right to attend college. Many women were well educated even though they had not had much schooling. Because teachers were scarce in the new territories, many women were accepted for the job. The county superintendent of education would give an examination to anyone who wanted to apply and from the results decide who was qualified to teach elementary school.

Many midwest teachers followed less formal methods than those of the traditional eastern and European schools. Bronson Alcott, the father of Louisa May, who wrote *Little*

Women and *Little Men*, introduced in Concord, Massachusetts, some ideas that were rejected as radical. But they were taken over by some schools in England, which set up Alcott House as an institution to train teachers in his methods. Count Leo Tolstoy, planning a school for his serfs at Yasna Polyana, explored schools in Europe, especially in Germany, but settled on Alcott's methods.

Louisa May's books illustrated her father's ideas. Many readers in America, especially women, approved of and followed them. Alcott's radical ideas included educating girls as well as boys and fostering the total growth of the child: physical, emotional, social, spiritual as well as intellectual. He also advocated following the recommendations of Agassiz that children should be taught to observe life around them and express their reactions in speech and writing. Alcott introduced field trips and other learning approaches that are commonplace now. Some of Alcott's controversial ideas are reflected in the experiences at Freedom School.

Sod Schoolhouse takes place during an era when immigrants steadily were settling the Plains and communities rapidly formed. People governed themselves in these isolated enclaves; to do so they had to be able to understand each other. The settlers survived by helping each other, and in the process they absorbed each other's speech patterns.

Because the people who settled the prairies came from many countries, and from many levels of education, the nation recognized a special need to help newcomers quickly learn what they needed to know to be self-governing citizens. For this reason the government initiated and promoted schools free to all residents, enabling them to learn to read, write and speak proper English. Schools were to be located so that every child could reach one either by walking or riding horseback or driving a buggy. They were usually one-room buildings with a shed for the coal, cobs for the stove in the winter, and feed for the horses.

PREFACE

Freedom was a fairly typical school. Bonnie Bess frequently visited cousins who were scholars in a similar school. Courtner experienced some of his happiest days in such a school, where many languages and customs mixed. Knowing something of the world in which the children who attended Freedom School lived helps *Sod Schoolhouse* readers understand and enjoy reading about a time and a way of learning that is much different from our own.

Courtner and Bonnie Bess
Brawley, California
April 1996

SOD SCHOOLHOUSE

CHAPTER ONE

School Days Are Coming

*U*NDER THE BLAZING sun of a scorching, cloudless August day on the Kansas prairie in 1875, two small boys dutifully chopped at a seemingly endless ocean of sunflowers stretching through the long, straight rows of corn. The corn was taller than the boys, and so were the hoe handles.

With the skilled rhythm of much practice, four sturdy arms rose and fell, whack, whack—and the sunflower faces fell, one after another, onto the black dirt.

"Whopper, this is!" the taller boy exclaimed. "Watch me, David! This sunflower is a giant, and I'm going to kill him dead."

"But Robbie, if he's a giant, I ought to kill him! Like Goliath, because I'm David!"

"Go ahead! Let's see you—with one whack!" David left his own row, attacking the thick green stem with new energy. It shuddered but did not fall.

"Yeah!" his brother taunted, "you're not big enough!"

"It's just because my durned old hoe is dull. It's wore down."

"Watch me!" Robbie swung fiercely. "Yippee! There goes that old Philistine!"

"You got Goliath, all right. The rest are the armies of the Philistines, and we are the armies of Saul—and I'm going to kill ten thousand!"

"You can't kill more than me—I'm going to kill a million thousand!"

For a spurt the hoes whacked faster and faster, and the smiling golden blossoms were cut off for several yards.

David slowed and stopped, exclaiming, "I'm thirsty!"

Robbie gave one more vicious chop, then pushed his broad straw hat back to wipe the sweat away from his face with the bottom of his shirt tail.

"Me, too," he agreed. "Let's dig up the jug."

Their bare feet hopping from clod to clod on the hot ground between the corn rows, they made their way to a pile of cut sunflowers left as a marker. One old corn-cob stood on end in the dirt. With his hoe Robbie scraped away at the loose soil. David, digging with his fists, brought up the stone jug they had buried to keep the water as cool as possible. Robbie took the jug, pulled out the cob that made a stopper, and tipped the jug upon his arm as the men did. He let a long, gurgling stream run down his throat, first inside, then outside. David waited patiently. David could not swing the jug, but with both hands he got it raised and followed his brother's lead in pouring some over his head.

Their hair, which had been shaved short at the beginning of the summer, had grown into thick mats: Robbie's straight and dark brown, David's curly lighter brown. The still-cold well water soaked in, trickling in thin clean rivulets down through the dust and sweat on their faces and necks. In the sweltering heat it felt sharp and delicious.

They looked at each other and laughed.

"You've got stripes, Robbie! You're a zebra."

"You too! You're a zebra, too, David. There's a stripe everywhere the water ran."

"Robbie, do you think there are real zebras, or are they just in books, like fairies?"

"There's real ones—Hartley said so."

"Where?"

"I don't know. Maybe in heaven."

"Do you suppose we'll find out when we go to school?"

School! It was a mystery that hung over them, coming closer and closer: threatening, fearful, the unknown.

"Father and Mother went to school, and they are all right, so I guess we will be, huh Robbie?"

"Of course. I'm not afraid."

"Me neither."

"Father went in Massachusetts because he lived there before he grew up and went to Indiana and married Mother—Phoebe said. Do you suppose our new school will be like his Back East?"

"Anything in Kansas is better than any old thing Back East," Robbie said firmly. "So ours will be better. Father says it shows what a good state Kansas is that it set aside land for every district to have a school. Now there's enough children in our district and we've got that nice white building and a teacher hired, and it's going to be good. Father says."

David carefully wrapped the white cloth over the cob, and fitted it back into the neck of the jug.

"If so many settlers had not homesteaded this year, maybe we would not have any school still. I sort of wish more people who left after the grasshoppers hadn't come back—or other people instead. I mean last year when the grasshoppers ate everything and so many people went Back East, I heard Father say it looked for a while like we couldn't have a school after all."

"Yeah. But Father and Mother felt awful bad. They had worked hard to get the district organized, and they said it is getting late for Phoebe and Hartley. They're getting old, you know. Phoebe is about to have her fourteenth birthday, and Hartley is past twelve. We got to think of them."

"I guess it's pretty bad to grow clear up and not ever have school, huh Robbie?"

"Sure, and even if Father thought they ought to just build a sod schoolhouse like Texas District has and spend the rest of the money to get a teacher with a first-class certificate, I'm glad old Mrs. Chisholm won the fight. She said she wouldn't have her children go to school in 'a old dirt building.' Well, a

3

soddy is nice, but our new house is nice, too, and anyway now our school is wood and painted white, and a lot nicer than those Texas kids got.

"Freedom School. That's a better name than Texas."

"And it's a better schoolhouse. Just think, it's got a well—150 feet deep, with water as good as ours. The Texas teacher has to carry water every day in a barrel, and it tastes awful. And we got glass in the windows, and they open up and that good shed for the cobs and coal for the stove, and plenty of room in the mow above for hay for our horses."

"I like the desks, the way they open up to put your books in, and only two people to a desk, instead of everyone on a long bench like at Texas. They have to hold their slates on their laps, and when someone is called to recite, everyone has to stand up to let him by, and they scrunch each other's feet going past."

"A lot of those scholars at Texas are mean."

The boys had drifted over to the hard-packed ground between the field and the hedge of Osage orange trees. Stepping carefully to avoid thorns that might have fallen on the ground from the trees they found a clear spot and stretched out on their stomachs. With a stick David began drawing pictures in the dust. Robbie, noticing one of the long, crooked cracks that formed when the ground got so hot and dry began idly scooping dust and scraping it into the crack. No matter how much dirt anyone scraped into one of those cracks, the cracks never filled up.

"Where do you suppose all that dirt goes to, Robbie?"

"Goes to China, I guess. That's on the other side of the world, Hartley says."

"That's where the men wear pigtails instead of cutting their hair, and they wrap up girls' feet to make them little. I remember."

"If Phoebe's feet were wrapped up so they'd be little, she couldn't catch us so easy."

"She just about can't catch me—I'm getting pretty fast."

"Not as fast as Hartley."

"No one's as fast as Hartley. What do you suppose some Chinaman's saying when this dirt comes falling down onto his pigtails?"

The boys laughed.

The little boys were still not quite used to the idea that they, too, would go to school. The first plans had been that their sister Phoebe, their brother Hartley and nine-year-old Tessie would go. Three miles was too far for the little boys to walk in the winter, and the Dawsons only had one spare horse, the gentle pony, Captain, who would be unable to carry five.

But then, late in the summer, neighboring Indians had given a beautiful palomino horse each to Phoebe and Hartley as a thank-you for helping one of their women and her baby. The two were lost in a snowstorm the winter before when Mr. and Mrs. Dawson were both away and the children were alone in the old soddy. Phoebe and Hartley had been frightened when the woman knocked at the door in the night, but they had taken her in and helped with her sick baby. Hartley had cared for her horse and then ridden him; before that he had never been ridden by anyone but the Indian woman. The Indians had all come to visit just a few weeks before, bringing the horses and hand-woven blankets. Now Phoebe and Hartley could ride their own, and Mother and Father had decided that Captain could pull the buggy with Robbie and Tessie in it.

But seven-year-old Robbie and David, almost six, could not stand the thought of being separated. After much talk, it was finally decided that David might as well go, too.

"You'll never have any peace with him alone, Mother," Phoebe said. "And Hartley and I will look after him."

"Besides," Hartley added, "every morning it will be a fight to get Robbie to go and leave David."

Father agreed. "Robbie is not so likely to get into trouble with David there."

Finally Mother kissed David and said they were right.

"It's just that it will seem so lonely with all of you away at once. So terribly quiet!"

"But you will still have Martha and Mary Ann and pretty soon the new baby!"

David still was not sure which would be worse—staying home without Robbie, or facing a strange teacher and all those new children. Sometimes his throat was so tight he could not swallow.

Robbie had accumulated a big pile of dust which he now swept all at once into the crack, laughing.

"Whillakers, that old Chinaman sure got it then. David," he added, "you know what I think? I think old Joshua is meddling with the sun again, you know the way he made it stand still, because I have been watching, and the shadows haven't gotten longer for a long time. It must be about suppertime."

"Sure seems like a long time. Look at my shadow—just a teeny smidgen. It ought to be a lot bigger than that, seeing all the time since dinner. But no one has rung the bell yet."

"Let's go wade in the crick, then start back from that end."

Carefully avoiding stepping on cockleburs with their bare feet and watching for rattlesnakes, they started loping with new energy down the row toward the shallow stream that bordered their homestead on the west. Their hoes, dragging behind them, bounced and slid over the rough ground in interesting patterns.

West Creek cut off a corner of the field, and along its banks a fair-sized strip of cottonwood trees offered welcome shade. Dropping their hoes, the boys held to branches and half-climbed, half-slid down the crumbly sides and into the shallow, cool water. To their hot feet it felt luxurious; they splashed back and forth several times. Then Robbie, stepping

6

gingerly on the rocks underneath, sometimes sinking into a squishy mud hole, made his way back toward the bank.

"You getting out already?" David asked in dismay.

"Naw—I just thought I'd take off my clothes so's they wouldn't get muddy."

"No one ever said we couldn't go wading."

"Course not."

Neither wanted to admit, even to himself, that they had any intentions of deceiving anyone.

Robbie, following his own thoughts, suggested, "We aren't quitting; we're just taking a recess, like Father says they have in school."

"And we aren't laying down on the job, because we aren't laying down."

"You're supposed to say, 'Lying down'."

"Well, it's the same thing. We're both standing up."

Having satisfied themselves with their own excuses, they carefully fastened their clothes to branches hanging out within reach, and in delight began splashing the cool water at each other. The mud was cool, too, and soon they were spreading it carefully over themselves and each other, feeling its smooth, soothing stickiness, wiggling against the coating as the mud began to dry on their skin in the hot, dry air, joyfully finding new pools and washing it off. They watched the thick brown pools surge up over their feet with each step, and then the clear new water from the slow current making little whirls and eddies of designs until soon, if they stood still, the water was again pale blue from the sky's reflection and darker where the leaves shaded it.

"It's pretty, isn't it, Robbie. Sometime when I have me some paints, I'm going to make a picture of it. Like those pictures in Father's books."

"Shucks! You couldn't make pictures like that. You have to be an artist in New York or someplace to make a picture like that."

"Then maybe I'll go—where did you say?"

"New York. And you won't go there. It's a million miles Back East and rich dudes live there."

"Oh." Sadly, David watched the mixing of the brown mud and the clear blues of the water.

Suddenly Robbie leaped high, pounced with both hands into the mud, and exclaimed triumphantly, "Got 'im!"

"Got what?"

"This big old frog, that's what! Help me make a corral for him with some rocks."

Obediently David scrambled to arrange rocks in a hollow pile. Placing the frog safely in the pen, they set one final rock on top to create a roof.

"David?"

"What?"

"Can you keep a secret?"

"Sure I can. Course! Don't I always?"

"No. You always tell."

"I won't, Robbie. Try me. I'll be mum as mum. Who's it a secret from? Not Father?"

"Es-pec-ially Father! I guess I better not tell you."

"Yes, you had—or I'll tell him."

"Tell him what?"

"Tell him you've got a secret you don't want him to know. So tell me. I won't tell—even Father."

"Well Heinie Pfitzer and me have got five frogs and two snakes."

"Ha! Some secret!"

"But you don't know what we're going to do with them."

"Well what are you?"

"We're going to take them to school."

"To school! That's dumb! You can't teach frogs anything."

"Who's going to teach them anything? We're going to put them around in the seats, and maybe in the teacher's drawer—and watch everyone jump and yell!"

David's eyes glowed. "Maybe someone will sit on one—like that fat Clausen girl!"

Both boys laughed.

But Robbie warned, "Be sure you don't tell! Heinie said not to let you in on it, because you're just a little tadpole, and you'd give it away."

"I am not a tadpole! I'm five going on six. Who's he, thinking he's so big? He's only ten—that's not much bigger than me."

"It's six years bigger."

"Is it?"

"I think it is."

"I guess we'll learn to figure at school, won't we, Robbie? And do hard problems about how much water in the well and how many bushels of wheat, like Father gives Hartley?"

"Sure. We'll learn everything."

"Robbie—do you want to go?"

"Sure. There's all those kids to play with, and we can play fox and geese, and pum pum pullaway, and king of the mountain and run sheep run—and on rainy days, poor pussy. And we'll have snowball fights in the snow. They're all more fun with a lot of people. And probably there will be some good fights, besides snowballs."

"You know Mother and Father don't want us to fight."

"Course, we won't start any fights on purpose. But if there is a good fight, they wouldn't want us to just let someone knock us around."

David squirted water with his fist so that it made a fountain in the air. Then he said, "Of course Hartley will be there. He wouldn't let anyone knock his brothers around like they do in Texas School."

"Just let someone try! Don't you worry, David. When Hartley has to stay home to help farm, I'll take care of you. Just feel my muscle."

Robbie made a fist and raised his arm, and David felt the hard little knot that formed below Robbie's shoulder.

"Yeah. It is pretty strong, I guess."

Somehow, the muscle inspection reminded them of hoeing, and suddenly they realized that the shadows of the overhanging branches were reaching far out into the creek from the west bank. They waded quickly to the deeper pool, had a final wash, inspected each other for telltale mud spots, carefully collected their clothes, and holding them overhead made their way downstream a few yards to the ford, where the banks were shallower and a wagon trail crossed. There they scrambled out, let the hot sun and steady wind dry them a little more, pulled on their clothes and started back to their sunflower assignment. Not until they arrived did they remember that they had taken their hoes with them. The distance to the creek seemed much longer this time, but when they found the hoes they also noticed the telltale footprints down the bankside.

"Like Robinson Crusoe," David pointed.

"Yeah. David, maybe it would be better to go back where we were working instead of at this end. After all, Father said to hoe up there."

Again they had drinks. Then, tired but a little worried, they worked steadily for a while. The shadows were getting longer, and the row of cut sunflowers was pretty short.

Finally David said, "Robbie when you think about going to school, hoeing sunflowers isn't so bad a job after all. You know they aren't going to do anything behind you when you aren't looking."

"Just let them try!"

In the Dawson family's old sod house, Phoebe sat on a low bench carefully stitching the hem of the new pink calico dress her mother had finished for Tessie; her own blue dress was pressed and hanging in her closet in the new house. As she sewed, her mind turned to the coming first day of school.

"Phoebe, you'd better call David and Robbie. I want to try their shirts on them before supper. Their arms are growing fast, so I made the sleeves long, but I want to tack them up enough so that they don't dangle over the boys' wrists—clothes that are too long look sloppy."

Phoebe carefully stepped over Martha and Mary Ann, who were sleeping on a blanket on the cool, hard dirt floor of the soddy, and through the open doorway as she headed outside to find her brothers.

The sun glared down from a brilliant blue sky through shimmering heat waves onto far-stretching prairies. Within the wide circle stretching from horizon to horizon on all sides, there were few clues that humans had touched the landscape: a few windmills, dwarfed by the distance; to the east, the low rise of the Moore sod house and their white-topped wagon, resembling a large mushroom; a discernible break made by a small grove of young Osage orange trees the Dawsons had planted. Otherwise there was nothing but seemingly endless stretches of parched prairie grass broken by small patches of brown wheat stubble and the field of corn to the west, where the Dawson boys were cutting the ever-threatening sunflowers.

Across the road from the soddy, the white painted frame house stood out. The only white spot in all that varying brown, it looked cool, but it was not. The heat beat through the shingled roof and the clapboard walls and glared into the sparkling glass windows despite the neat white muslin curtains. The old sod house, with its yard-thick sod walls, sod roof and deep-set small window openings did a much better job of keeping the sun at bay. For this reason Phoebe and her mother had taken their sewing over to the soddy.

Tessie had been making doll clothes from the scraps; now she followed Phoebe across the barnyard. Together they washed their faces in the cool water being pumped into the tank below the windmill before crossing the wide, dark-brown plowed strip of the firebreak that surrounded the buildings.

The stretching miles of high, thick prairie grass, parched by the summer heat, were always a fire threat. The year before, a few miles north, a raging fire had spread for miles. It had burned out several families and killed one young mother and her baby. Many badly burned horses and cattle, as well as antelope and elk, were shot in mercy. Every careful settler plowed several furrows around his buildings in hopes of breaking subsequent fires should they come.

But now the girls had crossed the break and reached the edge of the cornfield. Phoebe called, her voice ringing high and clear against the silence. Then the girls listened. But there were no answering shouts.

"Phoebe, should we ring the big bell?"

"No—too early for supper; Hartley and Father would hear and think something was wrong. We'll have to go look for them."

"Phoebe, listen to those meadowlarks! Wouldn't it be wonderful to be able to sing like that! I wish I knew what they are saying."

"I know one thing they are not saying—that they have to go to school."

"Phoebe do you wish we weren't going?"

Phoebe glanced at her sister's troubled face. Tessie was always quiet, but Phoebe had noticed that lately she had been more so than usual.

"Are you worried, Tessie?"

"Are you?"

Phoebe started to say briskly, "Of course not!" But looking at Tessie's earnest, trusting face, she decided to be honest.

"You really are getting to be grown up, and I'll tell you the truth. I wish like anything I didn't have to go."

"Don't you think an education is important, like Mother and Father say?"

Phoebe pulled up a piece of grass and nibbled thoughtfully on the tender end. "Yes, I guess so. I guess I just wish I was born educated. Or maybe that it grew, like hair and fingernails, and I wouldn't have to leave home and Mother and the babies, and spend all day with lots of strange people."

Tessie asked slowly, "Do you think Mr. Lancey is right, that girls should not waste their time in school because all they need to know is how to keep house?"

"No, I do not! I know Father and Mother are right, that women are people, just as much as men: Kansas has given women the right to vote in school elections, and Father says some day women will even vote for the president, the same as men do. Then women will need to know just as much as anyone else about government and everything."

"Mr. Lancey says it is wicked for women to vote. He says it is against the Bible, but anyway if the country ever goes crazy and gives them the vote, their husbands can tell them who to vote for."

"Well, I'd just like to see any old husband tell me how to vote! And it can't be against the Bible, or Father would not be for it, nor Mother. So I guess we've just got to go, and do our best, whether we like it or not."

Tessie held Phoebe's hand hard. "I'm not afraid, if you aren't. And anyway, I don't want to be like Mrs. Lancey, always hunching her shoulders and pulling back when her husband comes near and crying at home, like we've seen her. I want to be like Mother, and say, sometimes, 'No, Francis, you're wrong,' and have him see it my way and kiss me. But I'd want to be right before I said it."

"Exactly! So we go to school and then to college, and

when we know everything we can help decide things and have them come out right."

They found their little brothers, who had seen them coming and were hoeing vigorously at the armies of sunflowers. Phoebe, looking down on the boys' heads, spotted the caked mud in their hair that they had not noticed on each other.

"How was the creek?" she asked.

"What do you mean?" Robbie looked big eyed; David turned away. Phoebe laughed.

"I guess you know. You'd better confess to Father before bedtime so you can sleep without a guilty conscience. You're to go to Mother now, she wants to try on your new shirts. Give me your hoe, Rob. I'll cut a few. Father wants so much not to have them go to seed, and he and Hartley are terribly busy."

"Me too," Tessie took David's hoe. "I'll cut some."

"No, you'd better help Mother with supper. David and Robbie will help, too."

"Aw—getting supper is women's work!" Robbie scowled.

"And hoeing sunflowers is men's work but the men didn't seem to get it done. And when they don't, women have to pitch in and help. So I guess the men can pitch in to do what they think is women's work. Now shoo. Mother is waiting."

"I'll beat you there," Tessie taunted as she darted toward the house. The boys took up the challenge.

In a few moments Phoebe was alone on the great prairie, her own lengthening shadow the only sign of movement. With sturdy, steady skill she chopped swiftly down the row. As she sometimes did, she talked out loud as she worked.

"I hate to have to cut you down," she said to the waving yellow blossoms centered in rich brown. "You are pretty. But you are bad for the crops. Still, you grow right back through the hard dirt in the horrid heat, no matter how much hail or hot wind or grasshoppers, nor how many times you are cut. You are always shining back at the sun, looking toward the bright side. Always strong, always cheerful. Father says that is why we took you for our new state flower.

"I am going to be just like you. You'll see!"

SOD SCHOOLHOUSE

CHAPTER TWO

MEETING THE NEW SCHOOLMASTER

*T*HE FIRST DAY of school was the greatest event the new community had seen, and everyone went. The night before, all the Dawsons had their baths in the tin tub beside the kitchen stove. Mrs. Dawson and the girls had kept the new stove hot all day, frying chicken, baking bread and caramel cake and custard pies, and boiling potatoes for salad and eggs to devil. Tessie arranged on the good glass dish from Back East a large pat of molded butter, fancied with the whittled butter mold Father had made while he drilled the children in spelling and arithmetic. The boys brought jars of apple butter and peach butter, jam and sweet pickles and dill pickles from the cool storage in the soddy.

Clothes were laid out for morning, and the children wondered excitedly what school would be like.

They all woke and arose quickly when their father called.

"Beautiful day. A nice little haze, no wind. No rain," he reported. Phoebe boiled corn meal mush and fried side meat and eggs for breakfast, serving them with buttermilk chilled from hanging in the well. Hartley and their father fed and watered the horses and cows, milked, and fed the chickens and pigs. While Mr. Dawson hitched the team to the farm wagon for the rest of the family, Hartley bridled his own and Phoebe's beautiful golden riding horses.

At last the moment Hartley had been looking forward to forever was coming—he would ride his own horse up to the new hitching rail at the school, a man on top of the world.

"Father," he exclaimed, "I don't see why we have to go so early. No one else will be there."

"I hope not. As director of the school board, it is my job to be there to welcome the rest."

"Aw, shucks. No one will see me ride up."

His father laughed. "I see, you want to show off. Well, you could work around here a while and come later. But your mother has been counting on you to take charge of freezing the ice cream, you know. She is taking the cream, the Pfitzers are bringing sugar and the Cochrans will supply vanilla and eggs. Mike Garrett offered to bring ice from the railroad station. Someone who knows how will need to supervise the freezers and keep the boys turning steadily so the cream will be ready to set a while before dinner. I'll be busy introducing the teacher and talking with the others. I don't know how good someone like Gus Pfitzer or Gopher Martin would be at making ice cream."

"Yeah, they'd be sure to get salt in the top. I guess I'll go when you do, and then after dinner I might ride a little."

When they carried the foamy buckets of milk to the house, Mrs. Dawson had the four little children scrubbed and dressed in their best. Tessie, an old brown wrapper protecting her new school dress, was carefully washing the dishes already used.

Phoebe, with hair neatly braided and tied with bands from the material of her new blue dress, was packing food into crocks and pans and then, with old gunny sacking, into two large tubs. Everything was cool from being kept in the dugout cave overnight. Mr. Dawson drew fresh, cold well water, filled stone jugs with it and set them inside the tubs to help keep the food cool until dinner time.

Hartley and his father washed in the tin wash pans set on the wash bench outside the kitchen door, quickly ate the breakfast Phoebe served them, then changed into their good clothes. By eight o'clock the comforts and buffalo rugs for the children to sit on were all packed into the wagon bed. Mother and Father sat on the spring seat in front.

At the last minute Phoebe wished she were going to be snuggled in with the rest of the young ones in the back of the wagon. As much as she loved her new mare, deep inside she was still not at ease riding her. But she knew the others would laugh at her for being a fraidy-cat if she changed plans now, so with her teeth set in a firm smile, she stepped into her father's hand, swung her leg over Star's broad back and spread her full blue skirt as elegantly as she could over the bright Indian blanket. Holding the reins in her right hand, she quietly wound the fingers of her left hand into the flowing, creamy mane to hold on as Star danced her usual little sideways dance, springing up a little in a few bounces, before obediently following the directing pressure of the leather strap on her neck.

The prairies were not silent now. The windmill creaked and whirred in steady pumping sounds, the chickens clucked and cheeped, the sheep and lambs called each other as they slowly moved away from the watering tank to graze in a cozy herd, and occasionally a mother cow let out a commanding "moo" to a calf straying too far from the line of cattle eating its way slowly away from the milking shed. Even the pony, Captain, ran along the corral fence and whinnied. The boys laughed.

"Captain wants to go too," David said.

Tessie called to the pony, "You'll go every day after this."

"Everyone set?" Mr. Dawson called to the passengers cuddled in back. "Then—giddyap!"

He cracked the reins lightly at the stolid plow team. The wagon wheels added their own noises as the heavy wagon moved into the lane and south across the firebreak and toward the school. The route had been traveled so much the year before by former settlers—driven Back East by drought and grasshoppers—and by the new settlers arriving, that the waving grass still showed the distinct marks of the trail, leading almost straight across the prairies.

"One of these days," Mr. Dawson commented, "the way the country is building up, people will be settled all through here. With this new barbed wire that they are starting to fence with, we will have to go around on the section roads. Then it will be farther to school."

"It's already different from when we arrived," Mrs. Dawson agreed. "Just look—now there are neighbors in every direction. And we have a school for the children at last."

Phoebe held Star back to walk beside the wagon, but once they were out of the yard, Hartley called, "See ya!" and with a couple of kicks on Palomine's side, horse and rider were racing away so fast they seemed to be flying. Soon they disappeared into the haze of the horizon.

The rest of the family, chattering and laughing, joggled along the rough ground. Tessie started trying to imitate the meadowlarks singing excitedly, and the others joined in. Mother began, "Buffalo Gal," the boys pulled out pocket combs with paper to play the music and the rest joined in the singing. They were starting on "I Been Working on the Railroad" when a new sound broke in—a startling sound— the resonant, swift clanging of a bell.

"The school bell!" they all exclaimed at once. "Hartley is there already and he is ringing the school bell! For the very first time, there it is!"

In her mind, Phoebe could see Hartley with his hands gripped on the new rope, jumping up to let the full weight of his body help pull the bell back and forth to ring out across the prairies. It was a beautiful bell, larger than most, a gift from some people in Massachusetts whose son had been killed by the pro-slavery guerrillas just before Quantrill burned Lawrence. Their son had planned to homestead in this neighborhood, and his parents had wanted to help with the new school as a memorial to him.

The Dawsons began to spot other families. Wagons, horses and groups on foot moved from all directions toward the sound of the bell and the shiny white building that was now coming into clear focus ahead.

The Dawson wagon pulled into the schoolyard first, but close behind were the Moores and a couple of new families. As Phoebe started to turn Star in beside Palomine, already tied to the rack, she recognized her old friends, Marietta Stephenson and her family, coming from the opposite direction. With Star more steady now after the three-mile trip, Phoebe felt more confident and rode on alone to meet the newcomers.

Soon the yard was filling with new arrivals, grownups calling greetings to each other, strangers being introduced, children drifting off together, chattering or silent according to their mood. Some of the larger boys lounged around the shed door, sizing each other up. Old friends happily insulted each other.

"Where's the schoolmaster?" Mr. Moore boomed. He had the deepest, loudest voice Phoebe had ever heard, and he always seemed to be laughing.

"Abe Pendleton was going to bring him from Newton yesterday, meet the train, then come over here later. He thought he would not plan to come until nearer noon, so we could have a chance to get organized."

Jolly Mrs. Moore laughed. "Sure, 'tis a good thing for the children to see each other first. That way they can plan how they will play jokes on him."

"I tink on dis schoolmaster dey vill not play chokes," Mr. Pfitzer said seriously, his German accent strong as he struggled with the new language. "De letter said he is a strong discipline man. He vill make every scholar obey, like should."

"One thing," Old Man Cochran laughed in turn. "He should not run out of hedge switches. Them trees the Roosians set out back in '65 have shore done theirselves plum proud." He was squatting on his hunkers, idly whittling on a piece of leftover pine and looking at the straight row of tall trees that bordered the schoolyard firebreak.

"What do you mean, 'the Roosians'?" someone asked. But the men were talking about Texas fever spreading to the cows from the cattle driven through to the railroad, and they seemed not to hear the question. The man turned abruptly to Phoebe.

"You're the Dawson girl, aren't you?"

"Yes, I am Phoebe Dawson," Phoebe wondered how the man knew her name.

"I understand you folks are old-timers. Do you know what he means by 'the Roosians'?"

"It was a family came about the same time mine did—when this was a territory, and the free-staters were coming in from Back East. The Roosians did not believe in slavery or war, and they came to see about land for their friends back in Europe. They were just crazy about trees. They said their families had gone to Russia from Germany, to a place like this without trees. They dug up baby saplings from the old forests and planted rows of trees to keep the winds from the crops and cattle, and of course, the people, too. One time some of their kinfolk came to visit from Back East and all of them had a big picnic here on the school acreage—it was empty, then—and they planted hedge trees all around. All in one day! The trees were so little they looked like tooth-picks, and some people laughed. Then the man got bit by a rattlesnake, and the woman took her children back to Pennsylvania. The next year, growing up already above the prairie grass, were all these trees. The trees on the Roosian's old place were even bigger, and people saw how good they were for fences and for firewood. If you plant them close, they will turn cattle, and the *Wichita Eagle* says some have grown ten feet in one year. In a fire they make pretty sparks. They make a hot fire and they do give a lot of good shade. But you must be careful going barefoot under them—they have awful thorns. And the juice from the hedge apples can make your face sore."

"Thank you, miss," the man said politely. "That was a most interesting bit of local history."

Phoebe felt her face suddenly burning hot as she realized how much she had talked to the strange man, just as though he were Hartley or her father. She murmured "Excuse me" and turned, seeing that the girls had all gathered inside the schoolhouse and left her alone. She flew across the yard, her sunbonnet dangling by its strings, bouncing on the back of her neck. The girls laughed as she came up. Marietta, the Moore girls and a new girl about Tessie's age, with Tessie, were gathered near the cluster of little children, all of whom were holding hands and exploring up and down the aisles.

Maureen Moore teased Phoebe. "We saw you had a beau, so we got out of your way. My, he's handsome. What's his name?"

"Where's his place?"

"Is he married?" the others asked.

Flustered, Phoebe said, "I don't know. I don't know!"

"What did you talk about? Did he ask you buggy riding?"

"No, of course not!"

"Well, you talked about something—we watched you."

"We talked about hedge trees. He was very polite."

"Sure, and I'm thinkin' he was that. We saw him bow right from the waist, like a gentleman," Maureen and Kathleen said, laughing together.

Kathleen said, "I'm warnin' ye, Phoebe Dawson, you're my best friend, besides my sister, but if I get a chance to talk with him, it's not hedge trees I'll be talkin' of."

"Whist, Kathleen—you're too bold by far, and that's the truth," her sister scolded, but smiled as she did. "Come, let's choose our seats."

"Which is the girls' side?"

"The side we choose—we're here first."

They ran their hands over the shiny, smooth surfaces of the beautiful, new patent desk chairs, traced with their fingers the grooves along the top to hold pencils and slate pencils, and even felt the curlicues of the black iron braces underneath. Maureen slid into the back seat on the right.

"I think Kathleen and I are the biggest. We will take this, and you, Phoebe, and Marietta, sit in the one in front of us. Then sometimes we can change seatmates and talk secrets."

The other girls giggled, but Marietta said, "I don't expect to come very long—just until I get the children into the habit and settled. The big boys are home now but soon they will be going to Texas to buy cattle and drive them up, and I'll be needed at home. But Father said I should start, anyway."

Phoebe hugged Marietta in alarm at the thought of losing her, but Kathleen ran out, returning in a few moments with a bundle of much-worn books and a slate.

"We've the one slate between us, and a little one each for Sean and Ellen. We'll put them in the desks to stake our claims."

"I've got a *McGuffey's Sixth*, and a blue-back speller in the wagon. I'll put them in, too," Phoebe agreed.

Some of the grownups began to come in, inspecting the desks, peering into the big desk with drawers in the front for the teacher.

"Look at the nice hooks on the wall for winter wraps. There's a shelf too, so they won't have to put their lunch buckets on the floor," Mrs. Dawson replied.

"What do you suppose those empty shelves are for on the sides?" Mrs. Moore asked.

"Books, maybe."

"Not likely—room enough there for fifty books."

"Room for forty scholars—might be, some day, they'd have fifty books. That there pine table at the front is good for recitations. It'll be better than sittin' on the front seat and holding your slate in your lap like we did. This way, every class can gather round the teacher close and write down what he wants them to. Shows schools keeps improving, just like everything else."

In front of the whole room, so beautiful that it was awe inspiring, was the great new reed organ in its shiny walnut case. It, too, was a gift from Back East. It had high shelves above on the back with carvings and tiny rows of carved spindles that looked like doll fences along the fronts of the shelves. At waist height, a shelf lifted to fold back above a row of small, shiny black-and-white slabs. Above them were shiny walnut knobs with flat white heads and black words printed on them.

"What do they say, Phoebe?" Tessie asked, poking her head in-between Phoebe's and Maureen's.

Phoebe shook her head. "I don't know."

But Marietta read them. "Flute, Diapason, Cello."

"My, you're the smart one," Maureen said admiringly to Marietta, "and where does it make the music?"

Marietta explained, "There was an organ in our house when I was little. See, you pull out some of these knobs, and pump these foot pedals underneath."

Marietta carefully sat down on the paper-covered bench and began pushing, first one foot, then the other, on two large, square red-velour covered pedals on the floor in the middle. Then she pressed down one of the white slabs.

"Oh-o-o!" the children exclaimed over the lovely sound.

"These are called keys," Marietta pushed some more slabs, and different notes sounded.

"They don't look like keys to me," a voice behind them said. The group of grownups took over. Mrs. Chisholm firmly reached past Marietta and closed the cover.

"This is not a toy for children to play with."

The children were angry, but no one wanted to be reported as being sassy to a grownup. They would have waited until the woman left, but new excitement outdoors caught their attention.

"Schoolmaster's come!" The word went around as big and little poured out to inspect the newcomer.

Phoebe, delayed by Martha, was still in the doorway, three steps above ground level. Suddenly she looked right into the eyes of the man who sat in Abe Pendleton's buggy. Phoebe knew in that quick instant that she did not like him. She did not like anything about him—not his tall stiff hat or his too-tight store clothes or the yellow cravat around his neck. She distrusted the hard look of his chin, the sort of twisted look in his eyes and his hands, doubled into fists in his lap. Most of all, she did not like the sudden, pursed-up smile on his mouth when he caught her eye, or the smirky look as he tipped his hat.

Phoebe pretended not to see him, holding Martha in front of her. He dangled his long legs out of the buggy, stepped down and began shaking hands all around, repeating that smirky smile, bowing to the ladies, and patting the smaller children on their heads.

When Phoebe found her mother with the other women, setting up the dinner on the trestle-boards in the yard, she stayed so close helping that the other women several times complimented Mrs. Dawson on her helpful daughter. Mrs. Dawson smiled proudly. Phoebe did not feel like smiling.

The rest of the day seemed to pass in a blur of excitement. As always at a community picnic, there was more food than could be eaten. Men and boys with heaped plates stood or sat on the ground, talking. Women with little children sat on blankets or spring-wagon seats set on the ground. Big girls and some of the women went around with water and coffee. When everyone had eaten too much, when the ice cream had been served and pronounced a great success, the women-folks cleaned up and repacked. After they exchanged some of their leftover food with each other and dictated "receipts" for special dishes, the call went around that it was time for the meeting. Slowly the big boys reluctantly were gathered and herded into the building. Mothers gathered their younger children around them, like chickens around mother hens, while the older girls took their places with great dignity. Those who could not find seats leaned against the walls.

Phoebe, holding Martha on her lap, sat beside her mother, who had Mary Ann. They all sat a little straighter as Mr. Dawson took a place standing at the front of the room and calmly waited until all was quiet. Seated behind him were the schoolteacher and another man.

"Phoebe, there's your beau!" the irrepressible Maureen loudly whispered. Phoebe hid her head on Martha's shoulder as her mother looked at her questioningly. But Father was speaking.

"Neighbors and friends. We are all neighbors, and we are all friends, even though some of us only met today. Out here, a stranger is just a friend whose name you don't know yet."

Some of the audience nodded vigorously, and a loud voice said, "Amen!"

Mr. Dawson took a deep breath, then continued.

"This is a day we have all looked forward to, a day of dreams come true, when we meet together for the first time in our own schoolhouse. For a lot of us this is the work of our own hands. At last we can look forward to watching our boys and girls—free citizens already by birth in a free country, and thank God in a free state, but not yet free from the worst kind of slavery, the slavery of ignorance—we can look forward to seeing them expand their knowledge and their understanding until they know how to make friends of the greatest minds of all past history. They will come into their heritage from all those wise people, and in the process become great themselves, each in his or her own way.

"Some may become leaders. Certainly our state and our nation—even the world—needs wise leaders. But most will, of course, be followers, because that is the lot of most people. We pray that they will not be blind followers, but will learn to take seriously their responsibility in a self-governing country to understand the issues before them, to use their coming great privilege of the ballot to choose wise leaders, to support good laws, to make this the best nation and the best state in the world for all people and to begin, right now, by starting to show they understand the real meaning of their school's name, Freedom School, by making this the best school district there ever was."

Enthusiastic clapping and floor-stamping followed. He smiled, saying "Thank you," then raised his hand for silence.

"And now I am happy to present to you, the patrons and scholars of Freedom School District—Schoolmaster Jerome Judson from Indiana."

The schoolmaster smirked with elaborate head-nodding to all the audience. He stepped forward, his hands clenched, his jaw set. His hair was plastered in slick whirls on each side of the center part, and Phoebe noticed that a number of boys had appeared after dinner with wet hair showing comb marks and newly plastered whirls similarly on each side of uneven center parts. The boys smirked at each other slyly kicking each other under the cover of the seats. She could see some of the legs. She felt trouble coming.

Then the man spoke. His voice, which had been soft and simpering as he shook hands outside, was now rough and hard as he yelled loud enough to reach the road:

"I am happy to be an important part of this auspicious occasion," he began, "and I can promise all of you fine patrons of this splendid school that we will have a school worthy of this elegant building. I will see that the young vines are twined in the way they should go; I will keep the light of learning burning bright at all times, and above all I will maintain discipline. Fear not that I shall spoil with lazy indulgence the raw youth you entrust to my hand. I stand for law and order. I always done it, and I will here."

He seemed wound up to go on, but Mr. Dawson, his mouth set in a strange, firm line, suddenly stood beside the booming speaker, and said quietly, "Thank you, Mr. Judson. We are sure you will do your best. And now—"

Mr. Dawson stepped farther forward in front of the schoolmaster, who stood a moment with his mouth open before finally sitting down.

Mr. Dawson continued, "Before we are dismissed, I want to introduce to you another welcome guest—a young man many of you have met informally during the day. Perhaps you talked with him not knowing who he is. This young man, a graduate of the great Harvard College in Massachusetts, which has sent us many of its distinguished alumni to help develop our state, is a new professor at our new University of Kansas at Lawrence. He is acquainted with some of the good friends in the East who have sent aid during droughts and sent generous help last year when the grasshoppers destroyed so much. He is a personal friend of the MacKenzies, who gave us our excellent school bell. Those friends, and others Back East, are interested in our progress, and in particular about our new and growing schools. He is writing a series of articles on education in Kansas, and we are very happy to have him with us today. We hope he will return soon. Professor Elliott Carroll."

The other young man on the platform stood, smiled in friendly acknowledgment, and started to sit down again, but Mr. Dawson asked him,

"Won't you say a few words to us, Professor Carroll?"

"It's him!" Marietta and the Moore girls were whispering in awe. "It's your beau! A college professor! And a writer!"

29

Phoebe said "Shs-h-h!" She felt her face getting hot again.

She noticed how smoothly he moved—like Star and Palomine, she thought. He spoke softly but clearly, differently from her father, yet slurring his r's the same.

"Thank you all. I first want to thank you for the wonderful dinner and thank the young men who so generously let me help lick one of the ice-cream dashers.(This news led mothers to look at each other and frown and motion 'no' with their mouths). My thanks also goes to the lovely young lady who informed me so kindly about the dangers of hedge thorns." He smiled directly at Phoebe, who felt suddenly the same way she had when she almost drowned once swimming in the Walnut River.

"Your fine new school building is a great tribute to your goals and ambitions. You show that you are dedicated to mental and moral development. These have been the foundation of our nation, and of your state. Already you know, even you little ones, that life is not often easy; for many of you some things have been very hard indeed. None of us who lived through last year's drought and grasshoppers will ever forget them. But you have learned also that the good things of life are worth struggling for and that education for all is one of the most important of those good things.

"I congratulate you on your building, of course, but more on your determination, your idealism and on the fine group of young Kansans who will be the real school. For a school, in the important sense, is not the building in which scholars and teacher meet, but the people themselves who use it for learning.

"You young people—you are the school. May I echo the words of your wise director in hoping that each of you will successfully work hard to make it the best school in the land. When you have graduated from here, I hope that you will keep learning and come to your state university, which your wise state leaders have made free for all. I shall look forward to seeing many of you there. And again—thank you all."

Phoebe thought it was one of the finest speeches she had ever heard, including the preacher's and the men running for office. She managed to look up as Mr. Dawson called on old Mr. Cochran to lead the closing prayer, after which the group became a lot of noisy families gathering for the return home.

When the Dawson wagon had pulled out of earshot of the rest, Mrs. Dawson exclaimed, "Francis, did you notice that stuck-up Mrs. Chisholm who talked so superior at the school meeting about not having her children in a 'dirt hovel' when you wanted to start with a sod schoolhouse and spend the money on a good teacher. Did you notice that although they came in that fancy surrey with a matched team, she only brought jam sandwiches and cabbage salad and a little plate of cookies? Ellen Moore and I watched her unpack it. She sort of slipped them on the tables when they were already full and stacked high!"

Mr. Dawson laughed. "That shows what a good thing it is to have a school, Marian. It's a place to learn about people as well as other things."

"Father, if he is a schoolmaster, why did Mr. Judson say 'I done it'?"

"Maybe because he was nervous. Making a speech to a roomful of strangers, especially when they are your new bosses, is not the same as teaching a class of children. And some people who grew up with bad grammar slip back into it even when they have learned better. I don't know about him, but it is one possibility. We will have to remember that he does not have a first-class certificate; that means he still has some important things to learn. Plan to learn what he can teach and not pick up anything he may get wrong at times."

Supper was mostly leftovers and quickly over. Phoebe, after carefully hanging up her good dress, helped get the little children washed and ready for bed. It had been a long, exciting day and tomorrow was the first day of real school. As Phoebe drifted off to sleep, the memory of the young professor's friendly smile almost drove out of her mind the unhappy thoughts of the new schoolmaster.

CHAPTER THREE

THE CHILDREN TAKE CHARGE

*P*HOEBE DRESSED FOR school and packed five lunch pails with fried chicken, an apple each, thick jam sandwiches and molasses cookies. A jug of buttermilk that had hung in the well all night was wrapped in a gunny sack to be shaded in the back of the buggy. Robbie and David came to the kitchen looking surprisingly clean and neat, from their wet, combed hair to new shirts and clean pants. They were carrying their socks and shoes.

"Phoebe do we really have to wear shoes? While it's still hot weather? Whillakers!"

"I know. I would rather go barefooted myself, boys. But Mother says school is to civilize people, as well as to develop their minds. And part of being civilized is learning to wear shoes all year. So put them on. You'll get used to it."

"Do we have to?"

"Yes. Mother said. So hurry. We want to be early to ring the bell, and if Tessie has to wait for you, she will be disappointed."

Moving like snails, they sat on the kitchen bench and began pulling on socks.

"It's like putting your feet in jail. How can anyone learn with his feet in jail?" Robbie whined.

"Well, if you don't learn to do what you're supposed to, Robbie Dawson, every bit of you will end up in jail, so your feet might as well get used to it now."

Just then their mother's voice called from the dining room, "Phoebe—are the boys there?"

"Yes."

"Well, tell them not to wear their shoes."

The children were startled, but their mother's voice continued. "Ellen Moore said yesterday she was afraid her children would be embarrassed because they were going to have to start without shoes. You may have noticed the young ones did not have any yesterday. Ellen said they had to buy some windmill parts and they just didn't have the money until after they sell their corn. She was hoping the children would be willing to go anyway. I told her none of the little children would probably be wearing shoes until the cold weather. It's just a waste of good money, especially for boys who scuff them around so. She felt better. I know when we were getting started we could not have afforded shoes for you and Hartley if there had been a school to wear them to, and if our children don't wear them, the rest probably won't either. So everyone will feel better."

"Especially me," Robbie murmured, happily snatching his sock off again.

With the three ponies and the light buggy it was a quicker trip to the schoolhouse. Hartley tied the horses, gave them hay and drew fresh water to fill the school water bucket. Phoebe set out their lunch buckets on the shelf and hung up her sunbonnet. Smoothing her hair, she checked the children and looked over the empty schoolhouse with a new feeling of belonging. The boys, who had run around the building once, rushed in to ask if the clock said it was time to ring the first bell. They had been learning to tell time, but were not sure yet.

"Ten more minutes," Phoebe assured them.

"Phoebe, can we play the organ? Can we, huh?"

"You mean 'may we', and don't say 'huh'."

"Well, may we play the organ?"

"Are your hands clean? Very well."

She had wanted to try it herself. They took turns sitting on the long padded organ bench, the paper still protecting the cover. They pedaled and pushed down on the keys, pulled the different bars in and out, finding that the same keys made different sounds with combinations of bars. Soon they each had discovered favorite combinations. Robbie and David together made a sort of winter storm sound. Tessie pushed in all except 'flute' and was trying to find the song of the meadowlark. That was too hard, but she did find notes that sounded like a bob-white.

While Tessie was having her turn, Phoebe picked up the big *Smith's Geography* book from the desk. She looked at the interesting maps and wondered if she soon would know about the people who lived in all those different colored countries. She glanced at the *Smith's Arithmetic* book beside it; no problems there that looked as hard as the ones Father had been giving her and Hartley. There was the big Shakespeare book her mother had given, with the wonderful ghosts and fairies, and a book of songs from the Pfitzers. The words in it were strange—she realized they must be in German. Maybe someday she would even learn to read it.

She hoped there would be different readers. At home they had all the McGuffey readers—they were interesting, but she knew them almost by heart. Her mother said the people who wrote the stories in them had written lots of other things, and Phoebe longed to read some of the rest. Maybe now with families coming from so many places, they would have some different books and the children could trade. Maybe school would be nice after all.

Suddenly, the schoolmaster's harsh tones broke into her dreaming. She had forgotten all about him!

"Get out! And stay out of my schoolhouse until I give you leave to come in!" he shouted. He was standing over Tessie, who quivered and shrank away. Robbie and David ran out. Phoebe moved quickly to take Tessie's hand.

"And you, Phoebe Dawson! You are old enough to know better than to snoop, just because you found a chance to sneak in! You will learn better in my school, I promise you."

Hartley, unaware of the teacher, stuck his head in the door, calling, "Phoebe! Is it time to ring the bell? I am going to let Robbie and David—"

The schoolmaster exploded. "You're going to let them! I'll have you know, young whippersnapper, that in my school I do the letting. Now go stand with your toes on that mark!"

He had been striding back to the door, following the running children, who now bunched together outside at the foot of the steps. He pointed to a shallow ridge recently scraped on the dirt at one side of the steps, and Hartley obediently stepped forward until his toes touched it, Robbie and David holding his two hands.

"Back of him you imps. Stand in back of him and stretch your arms so your fingers just touch his back. Now you move when I tell you to! There. Now! Drop your arms to your sides and stay there until I give you leave to move. And you!"

He turned on Phoebe and Tessie, standing near their brothers. "Over here. This is the girls' line—biggest in front. Now don't let me catch any of you out of line again!"

David began to whimper. "Phoebe, I didn't mean—" but the schoolmaster yelled again, stepping close to him, until David shriveled.

"Quiet, you! Did I tell you to talk? Well, speak up—did I?"

"No."

"No what?"

"No, you didn't." David was crying now. Hartley and Robbie faced forward, but with fists clenched.

"No sir! Say it—no sir!"

Obediently, David whispered, "No, sir," although their mother had always taught them that it was ill-bred to say "sir" and "ma'am" as some people did.

The schoolmaster continued, "When I ask you a question, you answer. And when I don't ask you no question, you keep your mouth shut. Is that clear?"

"Yes," David answered, and then quickly, "Yes, sir."

"That's more like it. You will see. We will have discipline!"

Phoebe was determined not to cry. She dared not look back at Tessie, but she could see that Hartley was about ready to explode.

"I am the oldest," she reminded herself, and she stood straight, bit the inside of her lips, and when she caught Hartley's eye, she smiled a little. He stood tall then. David, his arms obediently at his sides, hunched his shoulder to scrape away the tears with his shirt.

The schoolmaster strode down the steps and across to the high frame from which the bell was suspended and gave it a mighty jerk—some minutes late because of his delay getting the children into lines. As the other scholars began arriving, calling excitedly to their friends, they were surprised to get no answer. The five Pfitzers and the four Lanceys, all boys, arrived about the same time, in wagons, and while the older boys tied the horses, the younger ones ran up with lunch pails and books. They looked at the Dawsons, standing in such strange positions.

"What is it? A game? Can we play, too?" Heine and Gustav Pfitzer cried, with little Abe Lancey echoing,

"M-m-me, t-t-toooo! I w-w-ant to p-p-play!"

From behind, the schoolmaster grabbed Heinie's ear, twisting him around by it.

"It's no game, you'll see! This is school, and we will have law and order. In my school you will learn discipline!"

As he fiercely repeated his instructions, the Moores arrived. Kathleen and Maureen held the hands of little Ellen and Irene, and Sean and Patrick behind them. Michael had let them out at the lane—he was to return the wagon and team to their father and then walk over.

Gopher Martin on his pony, and his little sister Hepzibah holding on behind him, made a wild dash the last few yards and into the schoolyard, yelling like a tribe of Indians. Before he knew it he was yanked off his horse and shaken until, as he claimed later, two teeth fell out before he knew what had happened. Hepzibah, stranded on the pony, whose reins were dangling, began to scream. Fortunately the pony, having had his fill of running, joined the other horses munching hay along the hitching rack. Hepzibah was huddled on his back, crying and peering through her tears, while the children, all now in rigid lines, tried to understand. Phoebe whispered to Maureen, now in front of her, "I don't care what he does. I'm going to get Hepzibah. If she falls off at the feet of all those horses, she's likely to get trampled."

Before she could think and get more frightened, Phoebe broke out of the line and ran. The schoolmaster, catching the motion from the corner of his eye, turned as Gopher Martin broke loose and ran to his sister at the same time. Perhaps realizing the danger in the situation, the schoolmaster said no more as Gopher ran to the horse's head and Phoebe put up her arms for the frightened little girl. Phoebe cuddled her and whispered to her a moment. Gopher tied the horse and slowly unfastened the big saddle and threw it over the top fence rail. The three then very slowly walked back.

"Enough dawdling! All of you! In line!"

When all were in rigid places, the schoolmaster announced, "When I give the signal, the girls will march in and stand beside their seats, starting with the tallest girls in the back seats. Girls will sit on the left as you go in."

Noticing the girls' dismayed looks, he snarled, "Ignorant as you are, I hope you know your left side."

No one answered, so he snapped, "Now! Left foot first girls, march!"

More or less in step, the girls marched up the steps and stood by their assigned seats, except for the little ones, who wanted to stop and cling to the older girls. But the big girls furtively hushed them and pushed them into place. The schoolmaster, yelling at the boys outside, at last gave them the signal. In the boys marched, dropping out two by two to take their places beside their seats.

The schoolmaster then made a one-man parade to the front of the room, and barked, "Girls sit! Boys sit!"

"Now," he held up his hand. "In my hand I have a pin. When I drop it, I want to hear it hit the floor."

He dropped the pin, and if those in back could not hear it fall, at least they could not hear anything else.

He nodded. "I think you are beginning to catch on. Now I will give you my rules, and I don't plan to spit my tobacco twicet. If you think you have to leave the room, hold up one finger. If you want to borrow a pencil, hold up two fingers. If you want to ask a question, hold up your hand. Don't whisper. Don't scuffle your feet. And don't squeak your slate pencils. You will do the lessons I assign and have them ready when I call on you for recitation. Anyone who does not do his lesson, I'll learn him what hedge switches are for. Keep your eyes on your book. Anyone who finishes his lessons, fold your hands in front of you and sit still.

"I will now read the morning passage from the holy scriptures.

> *"Woe to those who devise wickedness*
> *and work evil upon their beds!...*
> *Therefore thus saith the Lord:*
> *Behold, against this family I am devising evil*
> *From which you cannot remove your necks;*
> *And you shall not walk haughtily*
> *For it will be an evil time."*

His tone and look made clear to the children that so far as they were concerned, he considered himself the Lord, and it would indeed be an evil time.

"We will now sing "The Star Spangled Banner." Girls,

turn and stand—boys, turn and stand. Rows straight! Attention! Sing!"

He plunged in, his voice booming and harsh, coming only reasonably close to the notes. With his eyes glaring at them up and down the room and his arm waving in a right triangle in the air, he sang. They murmured, their mouths moving but little sound coming out. When he had polished off the last screeching "Land of the fr-e-e-e and home of the br-a-a-ve," he reversed his orders.

"Girls sit! Turn! Boys sit! Turn!"

And again the pin fell.

"Now. Those who cannot write your names and the alphabet, raise your hands."

A few timidly held up their hands in the front row. Others, including Robbie, David and Tessie, seeing hands going up, quickly raised theirs, although all three could write that much, and Tessie could write quite well.

But Wade and Bart, the Lancey boys who were almost grown men, and Maureen and Kathleen Moore, not willing to admit in front of the others that they could not write, kept their hands down. The schoolmaster then pointed with one long, skinny finger at Maureen, Kathleen and Phoebe.

"You girls set copy for all the scholars who can't write. Now pass all your readers to the side.

"You!" he pointed at Wade, "bring the readers to this here table. All you big boys you and you and you—," he swept the pointing finger along the back rows, "come up and get placed in the reader fit for you."

When Tessie's turn came to be tested for reading, she was so frightened she could hardly make a sound. The schoolmaster put her in the first reader, although she could do well in the fourth. As Phoebe, moving down the aisle to check the slates, passed Tessie, she saw large tears dropping off her chin and making little wrinkled spots on her starched pink dress. Remembering Maureen's fear that the schoolmaster would discover she could not read, Phoebe suddenly bent over and wrote on Tessie's slate, "Ask if Maureen can help you read."

Startled, Tessie began to protest that she could read better than Maureen. Then she caught Phoebe's sharp look, and understood. She nodded and erased her slate carefully with the neat cloth fastened to it by a string. She glanced around carefully at Maureen, in the back seat pretending to write, and then timidly raised her hand.

"Please—could Maureen Moore help me with my reading?" she barely whispered when called upon. The schoolmaster, who knew he had his hands full keeping the big boys under control, was happy to let the girls look after each other. With grown-up girls like the Moores and the Stephenson girl in school, it seemed only natural that they should teach the small children. With a return of his yesterday's smirk he agreed.

He added, "Since the girls are now behaving, I will permit all the girls in turn to go to the back seats and be helped by Maureen, Kathleen, Marietta and Phoebe."

Tessie slipped into the big seat between Kathleen and Maureen. Under cover of the desk, the big girls patted her, and she trembled less. Ellen and Irene, not waiting for turns, also went back. Their sisters had them sit in the outside aisle on the floor, where they could write or draw pictures on their shared slate without being noticed. The older three bent together over the first reader. Tessie pointed to the words one by one and whispered the names. The older girls whispered them after her, and the teacher had no idea what was going on.

Hepzibah Martin, Connie Chisholm and the others were helped by Phoebe and Marietta in whispers. The girls discovered that if they were very, very quiet the schoolmaster did not much care what they were actually doing.

Recess was indeed a welcome break. It seemed a million years coming, but at last the schoolmaster shouted, "Girls turn, stand, pass for recess. Boys turn, stand, pass. Girls will play on the south side of the building, boys play on the north side. No fighting!"

There was no fighting, but also no playing. They sat or stood in groups, grumbling, threatening. But at the sight of the schoolmaster going to ring the bell, all of them quietly found their places in line. All except Wade and Bart. They had disappeared. When little Abe Lancey discovered that his brothers had gone, he began to cry, and Jim Lancey wailed, "They left us and took the wagon!"

"Don't worry, Jim. We'll take you home." Hartley reassured him.

Abe sobbed louder. "B-b-but I'm a-f-fraid."

Jim added, "Our lunches is in the wagon!"

Hartley ruffled his hair and said, "That's all right. We've got plenty to share; David, you stay with Abe until he feels better."

David was ready to cry, but this was his first time being asked to help. He was a little younger than Abe, but he was a little larger, and at once felt larger still. He led Abe to a bare spot and together they began drawing in the dirt with sticks.

After recess was arithmetic. Hartley, Marietta and Phoebe discovered soon that the schoolmaster was helpless with problems other than the ones with answers in the back of the book. Hartley wrote out some problems on his slate like the ones his father had given him, and in spite of the schoolmaster's stern watching, somehow problem after problem spread to other slates, until each time the schoolmaster called a scholar to try out in arithmetic, he was met with a strange problem.

"Teacher," Chris Chisholm asked with wide-open blue eyes, "I promised my father I'd get you to work this for him. He's digging a new well, and he wants to know if he goes a hunnert feet and gets water at sixty-three feet, and the well is seven feet acrosst, how much water will he have?"

Gopher Martin's father needed a report on how much hay in a stack twelve by seven by eight, rounded on top. Michael Moore, scorning Hartley's help, said his mother could not figure how much butter from six cows that gave seven quarts of cream every other day.

The schoolmaster said it was time for geography.

"After this, scholars must do just the problems I give out in the book. Tell your parents I got so many dumb scholars I got no time for extras."

From then on, the arithmetic was drilling in multiplication tables, and the guzzintas—"twelve guzzinta twenny four twicet," the schoolmaster would drone. The children would drone it after him with sly giggles and rolling eyes.

There was indeed plenty of lunch in the Dawson pails for the Lancey boys, for none of the Dawsons had much of an appetite. But when Chris Chisholm went to get their lunch bucket from the surrey, he found two strange syrup buckets with "Lancey" printed on a scrap of paper twisted onto the wire bails. The Lanceys had not been forgotten—someone had sneaked back.

"Wade and Bart are the only smart ones in this school," Gopher said positively. "Let's all go home."

"Not us." Rube Pfitzer shook his head. "For dat we get vorse at home. Mein fater iss hell-bent all his boys get schooling, make someting off derselves—for dat he comes to new country."

Gus agreed. "He'd skin us alive if we was to play hookey just because the schoolmaster is mean. He expects a good schoolmaster to be mean."

"My father does not expect anyone to be mean," Hartley said, "but also he does not expect me to run away—especially and leave the children here."

"And the girls!" Pat Moore put in, "If you were askin' me, that schoolmaster would be likin' best of all to have all the boys disappear and leave him with only the girls. Well,

I'm not about to do it. My sisters are that mean and bossy theirselves sometimes, but yet—"

When the schoolmaster scanned the line, he frowned as he counted to himself. But he said nothing.

At the dismissal signal the students left, as they had entered, on cue. They did not loiter in the schoolyard. Hartley helped the little Lancey boys into the buggy with Tessie, David and Robbie; all the children huddled together with no pushing or joking. But as the buggy, with Phoebe and Hartley riding on each side, crossed the firebreak and turned around the corner of the hedge, Bart Lancey appeared. Riding a big work horse, he took one brother in front, and one on behind. The Dawsons waited to offer rides to the little Moore girls, who were walking with their big brothers and sisters...

"Pat or Mike, you could ride Star. Go with Hartley to supervise the buggy, and I will walk with the girls," Phoebe offered. The boys decided to play mumbletypeg to see who got to ride.

"Tessie," Hartley directed, "you go on. Let Captain take his time. I'll catch up with you soon. Robbie, David, you take good care of Ellen, Irene and Sean."

When the buggyful of little children had moved beyond hearing distance, Hartley said, "I've been thinking."

"Haven't we all!" Maureen interrupted, for once not laughing or joking. "I'm thinkin' it's the first and the last day of school of me life, and bad cess to the whole thing."

Phoebe and Kathleen put their arms around her. Kathleen, usually the quieter, now protested.

"Don't say the words, darlin'. 'Twill break the good mither's heart, and the father's, too, if we don't make out somehow. They've worked and schemed to come to this country, all the while countin' on our learnin' our books, so they wouldn't have to hear people callin' us 'Shanty Irish.' If we stop, the others will not be wantin' to go, the way they follow every blessed step we take. And who's to keep Pat and Mike and Sean from talkin' back with their fists when they're mad? Not that—that rooster! Just us!"

"But," Maureen was crying, "I'm the oldest in the place, and you're next. He's goin' to find out, we can't always pull the wool over his eyes. He'll find out we can't read or write, then he'll laugh and call us 'ignorant Shanty Irish' for sure."

Pat and Mike, leaving their knives stuck in the ground, gathered near.

"He does that and I'll curl his hair for him!"

"You see, Mike," Maureen turned to him, "it's fightin' you'll be surely, and what kind of reputation is that for the Moores to earn in a new country?"

Her voice rose in a wail, "I want to go home to the auld country, with the blessed green and the water. It's no good being stuck out in this dreary stretch of dirt and brown grass without a tree or a flower to rest your eyes on, nor mountains in the distance with their purple and gold and grey mists. Wherever you look there's only more of the same. I want to go home!"

The brothers scuffed their feet and looked away. This was new for them—the whole family always counted on Maureen to keep a good joke going and laugh everyone out of sadness. Phoebe suddenly realized how hard it must be for them. To Phoebe, this land was the only home she had ever known. She loved it and was proud of it even when there was drought, and when the hail ruined the wheat at harvest time. The fierce hot winds, the threat of cyclones and prairie fires—even last year's horrible grasshoppers; somehow, all were part of her world. But for the Moores, it was so different, so strange, they must indeed find it hard to forget their old home. She took Maureen's hand.

"Don't you dare let old Wormwood make you feel ashamed. I'll tell you, he doesn't know much himself. Does he, Hartley?"

"I'll say he doesn't! He used bad English half the time, and he's so ignorant in arithmetic." Hartley explained what had been going on in the arithmetic classes. When Maureen heard about the problem of Mrs. Moore's cows and cream, her crying turned to her own clear laugh.

Suddenly Phoebe had an idea.

"You know what? I think probably he doesn't know any more about geography than English or arithmetic. And you do! All of you know ever so many things—because you have been places! Just think—you've been to Chicago, and Boston, and New York and all those places in between. You've seen mountains, and an ocean. I can't even imagine hills so high you have to look up to them, or so much water you can't see clear across it, like they tell about. But you've been in a ship your own self, and felt waves. You've been in England, and in Ireland! Until I knew you I sort of thought they were just colors on a map.

"Now—" they all laughed as she yelled like the schoolmaster, "I bet if you think of some questions to ask him about geography, and do it without laughing, he will be stuck just as much as he is in arithmetic. Will you?"

For her answer Maureen kissed her. "I'll not promise about asking any questions—but I will come. Though indeed it hardly seems life would be worth the getting up in the morning."

"He's not here forever, you know," Hartley put in. "He's only here for a three-month term."

"And you think your father would not hire him for the next?"

Hartley looked at Phoebe, and then said, "I'm pretty sure. When they find out that he's ignorant—and we'll help them find out—they won't want to waste district money. But they have all worked so hard to build the schoolhouse and done without things to pay school taxes that they will be awfully disappointed if it just breaks up. They can get in trouble with the law, too. If there is a school, people are supposed to send their kids."

A general agreement ended the conference. The Moores and Phoebe walked on. Pat and Hartley raced across the prairie and soon caught up with the meandering buggyful of laughing, playing little brothers and sisters.

"Listen," Pat told them. "Hartley has something important to explain."

"We have decided," Hartley said, "we are not anyone going to complain at home, or tell them about the schoolmaster. Maybe he thought we were all mean scholars like some at Texas School. You know they fight a lot, and someone shot someone right in school a while back. Well, we'll give Mr. Judson a chance to find out we all know how to act right, and maybe he will, and be different. Now, we don't want to hear of any of you tattling, understand?"

"Sure, Hartley. I can keep a secret. Ask Robbie."

Ellen and Sean agreed, if that was what the big girls had said. And Irene agreed with them, even though she had no idea what they were talking about.

Thus it was that both the Dawson and Moore parents were surprised at how little the children had to tell about school. But they were not surprised, particularly, that feet dragged getting ready the second day.

"The novelty has worn off, and they are doing their duty instead of having one long picnic," Mrs. Dawson said.

The Stephensons were not back, but Wade and Bart were.

"Pa said if the state was going to steal money from him and call it school taxes, he was going to get his share out of it, and we was to come and stay, or he'd take it out of our hides with the buggy whip." Wade shrugged and spit tobacco.

Chewing tobacco was against the school rules, everyone knew, but Wade's father chewed constantly. Wade knew it was one place the schoolmaster would not get any backing. So, although he came back, he came chewing. Bart pretended to chew some, too, but it made him sick, so he always got rid of it when he thought no one was looking. The Dawson parents thought any tobacco use was a filthy habit, and Hartley did, too, but just now he was glad Wade liked it.

"If you get caught, and the schoolmaster licks you, your dad will be mad. And if you don't get caught, my dad will be mad."

"Oh, I'll get caught, all right. I reckon to see to that."

"Then if the schoolmaster doesn't punish you, my dad will be mad. So it's good either way."

Maureen did not ask any questions, but neither did the schoolmaster ask her any. She quietly helped and was helped by the little girls. Kathleen was not back. She was an expert weaver; her father had made her a loom, and a man had brought rags his wife wanted woven into carpets. The family needed the money, and Kathleen was happy, but it was all the more reason Maureen must make the best of things. The schoolmaster paid little attention until lunch period.

The fact was that he did not really think of her as one of the scholars, but as a grown-up who was coming to help little children get used to school. He thought she was not only very helpful but very attractive.

Maureen had been up since before dawn to help her mother with the washing, and she was tired, so when the rest of the girls started a game of pull-away, she sat on the steps. She pulled the beginning of a sock out of her pocket to knit as, from habit, she kept track of Ellen and Irene.

To her dismay, the schoolmaster, spreading his coattails apart, sat down beside her.

"How many are there in your family?" Mr. Judson asked.

"Ten children," she answered shortly.

"Ah, how splendid! A fruitful family in a fruitful country. And I'm sure you are the pride of the family." He laughed a little, trying to be complimentary but not too formal.

"No," she answered, knitting rapidly.

"And how long have you been here?" he plowed on.

"Not a year," The needles clicked faster and faster, until the creamy yarn almost seemed to run of its own accord.

"Indeed. And where are you from?"

"County Cork," she said, not looking at him.

He laughed softly, leaning toward her with a simper which was clear to the interested onlookers, including her brothers, who had run around the back of the building and were now peeking around the corner behind his back.

"Ah," he said, "permit me to correct you, my dear. It is Cork County, not County Cork."

At that the needles paused. Maureen's head raised up, and she looked off into the distance for a moment. Then, with a swing of her head, she turned and looked directly at the man—a look her brothers all recognized which made the schoolmaster draw back.

"Oh, oh!" Sean whispered to the boys behind him, "he'd better look out!"

"What did you say, Mr. Judson?" she asked in her normal, clear, firm voice.

"I—I said, it is Cork County, not County Cork," he smirked uneasily.

"Oh, it is, is it? Well, I'm thinkin' there is a lot of people I know will be glad indeed for that useful bit of information. And now, if you will excuse me, I must look after my sisters."

Calmly she folded her knitting, tucked it back into her pocket, walked down the steps, and left him with his mouth open.

"The likes of him!" she exclaimed as she joined the group of girls.

"Cork County, indeed! And to think I was ever so foolish as to worry about the opinion of him! Come, it's time to take up. I'll race you to the hedge and back, to stretch my legs." Away she flew, the others laughing after her.

The days dragged by. The older scholars continued to help the younger ones, and thus reviewed what they had already learned at home. The younger children, guarded by older brothers and sisters and by neighbors, began to get used to school. They enjoyed having other children to play with. They copied letters and numbers and drew pictures on their slates, they learned songs from each other at recesses, and they loved the stories Phoebe read or Maureen told.

It was the big boys who had troubles.

One morning Gus came in late.

"My horse got a sore leg," he claimed. Someone snickered loudly in the back of the room.

"You'll be sore, and it won't be your leg. Go out and cut a handful of hedge switches, and be lively."

Silently Gus went. Silently he came back—with five switches no bigger than a string. Again scattered laughter, as the schoolmaster turned purple.

"You'll pay for that sass, young man. Maureen, you go get some real switches."

Maureen went obediently; she returned with slips of trimmings no bigger than the ones Gus brought.

"The wood is so hard, my hands are not strong enough," she said calmly.

More furious than ever, the schoolmaster turned to Wade.

"You're strong enough. Go cut me some proper hedge."

Wade was gone a long time. The schoolmaster was torn between trying to watch through the window, which meant turning his back to the others, or letting Wade get away with defiance. But finally Wade came back with several real sticks an inch or so thick.

"Where you been?" the schoolmaster demanded.

"Hedge is awful hard to cut," Wade answered.

"Since it took you so long to do your errand, I'll teach you not to dawdle. Stand around here!"

Silently Wade stood as told. The schoolmaster picked the largest stick and flexed his arm. From the girls' side came the horrified protest, "He'll kill him!"

Wade grinned at them.

The schoolmaster, swinging the stick in an arc, yelled, "Let this be a lesson to all of you," and struck a mighty whack.

Crack! The stick broke, the longer part dangling on a thin strip of bark. It had been carefully cut almost all the way through!

In relief from their fear, the children laughed. The teacher turned on them all fiercely, but he could hardly lick the whole school at once. He breathed hard. Finally he ordered, fiercely, "Back to your work!"

When he dropped his pin, there was an epidemic of coughing and sneezing, especially among the small children in front. He had learned not to pick on them, because if he even yelled at David or Robbie or Abe or even some of the next ones, a fight was sure to break out in the back of the room that demanded attention.

When he sat down, he jumped up with a yell because there were tacks in his chair. No one had any idea how they had gotten there. When he opened his drawer, frogs and small garden snakes were likely to greet him. He learned to inspect his chair and his desk very carefully before taking his place, but while he was doing it, there were always giggles from all over the room so he could never tell who was guilty.

A mysterious little explosion in the stove was followed by a horrible smell that filled the building and forced everyone out.

Schoolmaster hastily jammed his feet down into his overshoes, to find they were full of water.

He no longer used hedge switches, but a belt which he hung over the edge of the desk each morning. Once he whipped Bart until he was sweaty, as Bart refused to give in. Pausing, the teacher strode back to the water bucket, took a big drink of water—and found it was so full of salt he spit it out. He looked up, to find the eyes of every scholar in the room on him.

Another noon, when he started to eat his lunch, he found nothing in the pail but eggs—cracked and rotten.

Then the books began to disappear. Sometimes they would show up again—and as mysteriously disappear. He searched all the boys as they left, and made the girls show what was in their hands. Every disappearance made him more determined to discover how the books were being sneaked out. He never suspected the high bustles under the girls' full skirts.

Since he could seldom find out who was to blame, he blamed anyone in reach. With each day's failure to improve discipline, he grew more and more furious.

Then he began to find little notes.

No two were alike. They were written or printed, in small or capital letters, correctly or incorrectly spelled. They never seemed to be by the same person but they were everywhere.

When he opened his record book, scrawled on the page was "Jerome Judson, stupid feller, has a backbone made of yeller."

In his desk drawer was "Teacher, teacher, can't keep school, teacher, teacher is a fool!" They appeared everywhere: in his pockets, in his hat, in his buggy.

The one that fell out of the Bible read, "This fool hath said in his heart, 'I am God!'"

At the moment he glanced up, again every eye in school seemed to be on him, every face seemed to know what he had just read. Yet in a split second, all eyes were dutifully on their books. He grabbed the strap but could not find any one victim to use it on. As usual, his face got purple-red clear to the slicked down curls on his forehead, and the veins stood out in his neck. But a very quiet school studied away.

Several times Mr. Dawson and the other members of the school board had dropped in for a short visit, but each time, all seemed to be a perfect school. The Dawson parents, among others, were uneasy. Their children had changed, but not in the ways that had been expected. The children said little about school, answered questions politely but vaguely.

"What did you do in school today?"

"Lessons, same as always."

"That's nice. What lessons do you like best?"

"They are all about the same."

And so it went. The Dawsons and the Moores told each other that the children now just had new interests, they could be expected not to talk so much at home. They did not complain.

Mrs. Dawson sometimes cried at night.

"It seems like I've lost all the children—even the little boys," she explained to her husband. "But I am sure it is good for them to grow more independent. They need outsiders. I don't want them to be mama's boys. Still—" and she would wipe her eyes.

Mr. Dawson said, "Marian, I don't like it. There's no other word for it—the children are getting sneaky. And I despise a sneak. You know I have distrusted that schoolmaster. But Martin says he has not had any complaints, and Pfitzer says I am looking to find fault because I wanted a first-class teacher instead of a fancy building.

"But when I come up to any of the children talking, they stop at once and go off in different directions. When I just ask a friendly question, they grunt some sort of meaningless answer.

"The worst of it is they quarrel and snarl among themselves as they never used to do. Oh, Hartley and Phoebe sometimes would get sharp with each other, or David and Robbie—or Hartley and Gus or Gopher—the usual children's friction. But this is different."

Mrs. Dawson threw her arms around his neck and held on. "You, too? I thought I was getting nervous and silly, or something. But if you have noticed too ..."

She sat up in bed and announced briskly, "We must do something."

But what? Like all the families with children in school, the parents had extra chores to make up for the work the boys and girls no longer had time for. But Mr. Dawson began to get a little news here, a suggestion there. He saw the Lancey boys, the Pfitzer boys, and once Chris Chisholm, in turn, with welts and bruises. Each said he had fallen, or been wrestling with a brother, or been thrown from a horse.

Mr. Pfitzer reckoned the schoolmaster licked the boys a lot, but he reckoned any teacher would.

Mr. Lancey said if the schoolmaster licked them, it saved him the trouble, because since the first day his boys had gone regular with no complaints.

Mr. Dawson asked each of his children if the teacher had whipped them, and each said "No."

It was true. The schoolmaster had early heard that "Old Man Dawson" never licked his children, didn't believe in it. Since Mr. Dawson was director of the board, Mr. Judson had managed not to touch any of his children.

"Hartley," his father asked, "are you afraid of your teacher?"

"No!" Hartley answered firmly.

Later, Phoebe asked, "Hartley, did you lie to Father?"

"No, I didn't. I'm not afraid of the teacher."

"Sometimes you look afraid."

"To tell the truth, I am so afraid I get to feeling sick at my stomach. But not of the schoolmaster. What I'm afraid of is that when he does get to me I won't take it like a man like the others have. They're all used to being hit—sticks, whips, straps, fists—I'd just die if I knuckled under, or cried."

Mrs. Dawson found Phoebe crying as she packed lunches. In the lessons the family always shared in the evenings, first Tessie, then Phoebe and Hartley seemed to be going backwards in things they had learned long before—multiplication tables, spelling, state capitols. And they no longer wanted to study at night.

"Don't we have enough school all day?" Hartley protested impatiently in a voice he never formerly would have used with his parents.

Then Hartley missed the slop pail as he poured out his wash water, and Phoebe snapped at him, "Look what you're doing, dumb ox!"

"I suppose you are perfect, Miss Know-it-all!"

He stomped out, muttering. "I've had about enough. I'm going to join up with the cattle drive to Texas."

"Oh, Hartley I'm sorry!" Phoebe called after him.

But he had gone.

Nerves were getting frazzled.

And then something terrible happened.

The day went routinely, until the schoolmaster, sure that Wade was missing reading words on purpose, cracked his knuckles with a ruler. Wade looked him in the eye, rose and returned to his seat without asking or receiving permission. The teacher ordered him back. Wade smiled, and sat still. The teacher yanked him out and strapped him. But the children were paying less attention. They were getting used to being hit, and watching each other be hit. Still, the tension in the room built.

Mr. Judson went for a drink, sipping it first cautiously, remembering his earlier experience. As soon as he finished, Bart went for a drink. He, too, sipped with exaggerated caution. Hartley followed, then Mike, Pat, Gus Pfitzer, Chris Chisholm, Gopher Martin. Each of them, one at a time, with great caution sipped and smelled before drinking deeply, and then quietly returned to his seat. When Heinie Pfitzer followed Gopher, the teacher exploded.

"In your seat! There will be no more going to the water bucket today!"

That was so completely unfair that the whole school gasped. Immediately, the little children began to be thirsty. They started going to the big girls, who by now were recognized monitors, asking if they must stay away from the water bucket, too.

Maureen answered Ellen in a voice that carried.

"Yes. Don't go near the bucket even if you're falling on the floor with thirst."

Phoebe kissed little Hepzibah, who was starting to cry, and whispered to her to be brave and go back to her seat for a bit.

Soon David started for a drink, got near the bucket, and Hartley reached out and grabbed him roughly and shoved him back toward the front of the room. David began crying, but silently.

The pin could have been heard, now, but the schoolmaster did not drop it. He sat nervously in his chair, then rose, walked toward the recitation table, but did not call anyone to recite. All the older scholars had their eyes glued on their books or slates. All the younger ones were watching with resentful eyes. He busily pulled out his record book. Out of it fell a large piece of paper, with a picture of a cross-eyed man with a center part, with two side curls twisted into very tight corkscrews standing up like horns. In yellow at the bottom was printed, "They used to say the Devil had two horns beside his head, but then he started teaching school and grew two curls instead." The schoolmaster, suddenly purple-faced and panting, jumped from his chair, grabbed his strap, and glared out over the room.

It was silent as death except in the very back, where Robbie Dawson and Abe Lancey had been sent to stand facing the wall for whispering. Robbie held a sheet of paper against the wall, which Abe marked on with a fat, yellow crayon. Absorbed in their picture of a sunflower, the boys were forgetting their troubles, and with them the rest of the school.

When the schoolmaster spied that yellow crayon, he shoved the hateful picture and poem into his pocket, and swinging his doubled strap, he almost dived down the aisle toward the unsuspecting little boys.

Hartley started up. Wade yanked him back, whispering, "Wait! One swat!"

Hartley understood. Once that strap hit a little child, they had the teacher for good. He was poised to be sure there was not a second one, and so was Wade.

But as the raging man almost ran down the aisle, he unexpectedly lurched and fell heavily forward. Angry as he was, habit had made him wary of the big boys. He had gone down the outside aisle on the girls' side, and when he reached Phoebe, she stuck out her foot and tripped him.

"Get him, boys!" Wade shouted, sprinting around the stove and sitting on the teacher's head. Quickly all the other boys were on the fallen man like a swarm of bees. Wade took off his own belt and handed it to Mike, who fastened it around the ankles. Another belt appeared for the wrists, which were strapped together behind his head.

"He's bleeding," Maureen cried out.

"What do you know?" Wade jeered. "He really has blood! I thought it was skunk oil running around inside of him!"

"Now what?" Bart asked, as Phoebe and Maureen brought towels soaked in water and held them to the bleeding nose. The teacher began to curse, and Maureen promptly stuffed her towel into his mouth.

Wade said, "Leave him here, and we'll all go home."

"No," Hartley said quietly. "This is our school, and he is not going to drive us out of it. He needs to cool off. Let's take him to the creek."

In a rush of enthusiasm, all the boys wanted to help.

Hartley pointed, and named the little ones.

"David, Robbie, Abe, Chris—you stay here and help clean up the mess. Pat, you and Rube get that door they used for a picnic table from the shed. We will pile him on it, and all help carry."

Wade said, "He's not heavy. Bart, me, Mike and Rube are about the same size—we can carry even. That's enough."

Hartley said firmly, "I think just the same it's better if everyone but the little children were in on this."

Pat agreed. "His pa's the director. And Gopher's pa is on the board."

So the tall boys, three on a side, carried the door, but the other boys had their hands on it. Even Chris Chisholm was finally included, because he was the only boy from his family.

Hartley looked toward Phoebe, who nodded at him in strong approval. Maureen was herding the littler children, some of them crying and clinging to her skirts. Phoebe, with determined steps, marched to the front of the room, opened the unused organ, pulled out all the stops and pumped hard. Then she started pushing down one key after another. It did not make music, but it made a noise, and it was different. Quickly, the younger children allowed Maureen to shove them into a half circle facing the organ.

Phoebe, still pumping the organ, ordered, "Sing!"

Maureen, whose voice was lovely, true and high sang out, "Skip-to-my Lou, my darling!"

Phoebe stopped playing the organ and joined in. Others followed. When they finished that they sat on the floor and went on singing until the big boys returned, breathing heavily. They were muddy and quiet but smiling.

At the sight of them, Robbie broke out of the song circle to ask, "What did you do with him? Is he coming back?"

Wade laughed breathlessly. "Not right away. Not right away."

The other boys laughed too.

"We buried him," they said.

Phoebe, alarmed, turned to Hartley.

"Alive?"

Hartley laughed again. "Pretty much. Don't look so worried. We buried him, all right—but just up to his neck in mud in the creek. We thought he needed to cool off, so we dug a long place in the mud and just plopped him in and covered him over. We took off the straps at the last and fast dumped some more mud on him. Everyone needed their belts back! Just his face was sticking out. It will take him a while to dig himself out, and he won't be in much condition to come back to teach any more school this day."

"School is over for today, I reckon," Wade said. "Come on, Abe."

"No!" Phoebe and Hartley exclaimed almost together.

Phoebe went on, "We said he was not going to drive us out of our own school and school isn't out until four, like always."

Pat said, "Let's go on without him. We heard singing as we came. We could do some more."

"Let's stay!"

"The big girls can teach."

"How about it, Wade?" Bart asked.

Wade looked around and then grinned.

"Suits me. I'd rather have Maureen for a teacher any old day than that ..."

"Mud turtle?" David suggested. They all roared. And when Wade sat down and folded his hands neatly in front on his desk, the rest laughed again and were soon in their places.

"Now!" Phoebe said laughing, "school can really begin."

CHAPTER FOUR

MR. GOULD STEPS IN

"NO MORE SCHOOL for now," Mr. Dawson announced that evening. He at last had been told about the children's experiences with Mr. Jerome Judson, leading up to the boys' burying the man in the mud.

"You should have told me sooner," was all he said. He borrowed Pal from Hartley and left to talk with the other board members and then with the schoolmaster.

"Did you see him?" the children asked when he returned. They had waited uneasily, wondering whether Mr. Judson had learned a lesson or would be trying to get even.

"No—and I don't think we will see him again. He walked across the fields to the Pendleton's where he changed and demanded to be driven to Newton to get the train. He told Pendleton he had an accident. Pendleton suspected something more was up, but he was glad to get rid of him. Judson's feet were sore from walking in wet boots, but he was afraid of rattlesnakes, so he wouldn't take the boots off. Pendleton hitched up and took him right in—said Judson could wait until morning in the depot. Mrs. Pendleton said she was glad to see the last of the man."

"I hope the next teacher is not like him," Tessie said.

"I don't know whether we can find a 'next teacher', Tessie. Teachers are scarcer than hen's teeth, and we aren't paying but fifteen dollars a month; a good teacher with a first-class certificate can get twice that. We had to have a fancy building and skimp on salary and this is the result."

"Don't blame yourself, Francis," his wife said. "You were out-voted."

"I don't think I will be out-voted this time. We must have a teacher who is educated and who has had some training in how to teach. About all Judson had was experience. Ten years of experience can mean ten years of doing things the wrong way. I say we need a real teacher or none at all—and no one disagrees. Sally Chisholm is in hysterics, and Jennie Martin is on the warpath after she heard about little Hepzibah on the horse the first day. The women are really up in arms, I gather. But the men agreed, too. Even Pfitzer."

"Well, where do you start looking?"

"I am going to write to that young professor from the state university and see if he has any suggestions. Martin thought he might have a line on someone who would fill in. If not, we'll just have to wait."

"And pray."

He smiled. "Yes, Tessie. But pray that we get a good teacher—not that there is no more school."

Phoebe thought guiltily that he had been reading her mind. But she was grateful for the let-up.

The next morning, drizzling and chilly, seemed to be the beginning of a beautiful day. Phoebe thought of familiar chores the family could do together with no worry about what the schoolmaster might do next.

She was happily digging potatoes in the garden when she heard Robbie and David excitedly calling. Still nervous, she dropped her spade and ran toward the sound of their voices at the front gate. Each of the smaller boys grabbed Hartley's hand as he loped from the barn.

"Come see the horse! Someone is here!"

The four of them rounded the house and stopped in admiration. Actually, there were three horses tied to the hitching rack, but one was just Mr. Martin's pinto, and one was Mr. Pfitzer's old plug in the buggy shafts. The third was the special horse.

It was a delicate looking springy sort, shiny black with white stockings. It was different from any horse that they had ever seen. And such a saddle!

"Look! Instead of a real saddle, he's got sort of a leather handkerchief," David exclaimed.

"No saddle horn! No lariat!" Robbie added.

Phoebe told them, "It's an English saddle. They use them Back East just for riding. Marietta Stephenson's family had one, but that's not it."

"Whose do you suppose it is?"

"Let's go see."

"I'm not going in all muddy like this," Phoebe looked at the potato field mud on her shoes and hands. "We can go in the kitchen and wash and then see."

"Aw, you're forever wanting to wash!"

But the boys submitted. Robbie, who finished first, ran to peek through the crack of the open door between the dining room and the parlor. He beckoned the others to join him. One above the other, with David sitting on the floor, they could see the group in the parlor: Mr. Martin, Mr. Pfitzer, their father and mother and a stranger. He was a young-looking man with black hair in a wave that flowed back from his high forehead. He wore an elegant tweed jacket and dark pants that fit into shiny brown tight-fitting high boots. He spoke in a clear, pleasant voice, his words running together, with soft r's like their father's.

"Frankly, Mr. Dawson, I have no desire to teach school—yours or any other. I came out West to study the land situation first hand, and to become more familiar with the local land laws. I am to take my examinations for the Massachusetts bar in the spring, and then I am to help supervise the legal aspects of the land holdings of my family's railroad.

"However, in some measure your problem is part of our problem. Our government grants are not much use unless we can get settlers to develop the country. Without settlers with crops to ship, the railroad has no business. But the kind of settlers who are profitable from our point of view, the kind who are determined, successful farmers, are concerned about education for their children. It gives an area a bad reputation if the citizens already there are so lawless that they cannot even maintain schools. As a result, if you think I can help, I am willing to temporarily, but only temporarily."

"May I ask about your own education, Mr. Gould?"

"Phillips Andover Prep, a year in both Switzerland and Germany, then Harvard and Harvard Law," the young man said casually.

"What's philipsandoverprep?" Robbie whispered, but Phoebe put her hand over his mouth.

"Strictly male, I take it," Mr. Dawson commented. "You know that Kansas schools are for girls, too."

"I suppose if they are capable of learning anything, they are able to learn the subjects of the lower forms. Mr. Bronson Alcott of Massachusetts insists that females are quite capable of all sorts of education but of course, he is a radical. Concord closed his school.

"I have no objection to the girls though I must make clear I have no intention of dealing with boorish hoodlums. I would be the first to agree that a young man of twenty or so without intellectual development is a dangerous animal, but I do not fancy myself an animal trainer. I should think fighting Indians or driving cattle or some such occupation would be more suitable for them than attending school. And I certainly am no infant nurse. Little children who need their noses wiped should have dame school of some sort, I should think. But for the children who are somewhat civilized I will offer instruction, if you wish, in the interim until you can secure a professional teacher so that the school does not have to be closed."

"Vat you tink, Dawson?" Mr. Pfitzer asked.

Their father's voice sounded somewhat strange as he

64

answered slowly, "I think that if we keep out the big boys and the little children, we will have a very small school. However, I agree that there is some point in keeping it open."

"I was thinkin'," Mr. Martin spoke up, "if the older girls, your Phoebe and the Moore's girls, are going, maybe Mr. Gould would be willing to let the youngsters go and have the girls look after them. From what I get from Gopher—my son, Edward," he explained to Mr. Gould, "the girls done most of the teachin' of the little ones anyway. It would keep the children in the habit of goin'. That's a good thing in itself."

"There is also the matter of the law," Mr. Dawson said pointedly.

"Legally, schools are free to all residents ages five to twenty-one. I think we might make a case for excluding the big boys on the grounds that they disturbed the peace. The young ones, though, I don't know."

The young man laughed, rather pleasantly, showing beautiful white teeth.

"I suppose one could try. The entire prospect is really quite strange to me, quite an adventure. So I will leave the arrangements to your judgment."

"Suppose, then, we start by keeping out the boys over sixteen."

"My Rube and Frank," Mr. Pfitzer said sadly.

"We will ask the older girls to look after the physical needs of the little children. And if you have any complaint about any scholar, you let me know," Mr. Dawson concluded.

"Very well."

"One more thing," Mr. Dawson suddenly added.

"I think it only fair to state that from all we have been able to find out about the recent trouble, the scholars put up with a great deal from an ignorant bully because they did not want the school to close. The big boys, whom you term 'hoodlums,' were strapped by him again and again, although any one of them probably could have bested him in a fight. When they finally rebelled, it was to protect very young boys, those whom you yourself described as 'infants' of five or six. I don't have a high regard for physical force as a means of regulating human behavior myself. But neither do I have a high regard for anyone who does not protect the weak.

"And another thing. At the age when you and I were being taught by educated men who set a good example to imitate, these young men were helping their families survive in a harsh and crude fight with the elements. If they are not yet intellectually developed—'civilized' I believe you said—let us hope, for the sake of our country, that their opportunity has merely been delayed, not permanently forfeited, any more than Abe Lincoln's was. You remember, he said that when he came of age forty-six years ago he had only gone to school 'by littles'—a little now and a little then—altogether less than one year. He could read, write, and cipher to the rule of three, and that was all. But my wife's relatives, who were his neighbors in Illinois, claimed he never was slow to stand up for the weak. In another fifty years, who knows what some of our seeming 'hoodlums' might become?"

Hartley and Phoebe vigorously shook each other's hands in silent pride. Their father sounded just as good as the other man and he used just as many big words.

Mr. Martin and Mr. Pfitzer had been nodding in approval. Mr. Gould did not answer for a moment. Then, in a different tone, he said, "I admit I did not think of it exactly like that. Perhaps I was condescending. However, in all honesty, I am sure I am not capable of coping with them. You can tell them I am a coward, if you wish," he said, laughing.

"He doesn't look like a coward," Robbie whispered.

"I am certain if they came, especially after their recent

experiences, more harm than good would be done. I know something of the reports of these frontier schools, and as I said, I am not a teacher. But what I think I can do, I will try to do."

Mr. Dawson sounded more natural as he shook hands and said, "No one can ask more than that, and we appreciate your help. I should add that my son, Hartley, although not yet sixteen, was one who helped bury the schoolmaster. If you wish, I will keep him home."

Phoebe squeezed Hartley's hand in alarm, but the man shook his head.

"No, let him come. Whatever you men think best. We will take it one step at a time, and see what we all can learn."

The grownups stood, and the children scampered quickly through the kitchen and around the house to watch the guests leave. The new schoolmaster bowed gracefully to Mrs. Dawson, shook hands with the men, stepped into the tiny stirrup and sprang lightly onto his horse. The horse pranced a few steps, then smoothly, one foot at a time, skimmed down the lane.

"Look how straight and easy he sits, like he was in a rocking chair," Phoebe said admiringly.

"Pooh!" Hartley scoffed. "I bet Pal could beat him any day."

"Maybe—but could you ride as elegantly?"

The children tried to look surprised when their father told them school would start again Monday morning.

"I hope you all will do your best," he added. "This is a man who can teach you a great deal if you will let him. He is doing us a favor by helping to keep the school open. I'm afraid he thinks we are a pretty savage lot. I hope you can change his mind."

Once again, the Dawsons arrived at school early. But this time they did not go in, although it was October, and the early morning wind was cold. As the other children arrived, the Dawsons spread the word of what they had learned of the new schoolmaster.

"Stuck-up aristocrat!" Chris said scornfully.

"I guess we'll show that eastern dude we're as good as his kinfolk, huh, Hartley?" Gopher Martin added.

"Sure, if he doesn't think we're civilized, we'll knock him down and prove it to him," Sean said, laughing. Without Pat and Mike around, he felt much older.

"Here he comes," called Robbie, who was perched on the roof as lookout.

Phoebe and Maureen called to the children. Happy to be together again, they remembered to line up quickly.

So it was that as Mr. Gould, on his dainty black horse, rode into the schoolyard, he saw two rigid, silent lines of children standing on either side of the steps leading into the white-frame building: girls on one side, boys on the other. He sat for a moment inspecting them. No one made a sound. Finally he spoke. "Good morning."

Silence filled the room. Everyone's eyes stared straight ahead. Then Phoebe, remembering her mother's way, said, "Good morning."

The man sprang down easily. His horse stood motionless. The man's clothes were different than those he had worn to the Dawsons, but they were of the same style—a blue jacket this time, and dark blue pants, with a shiny white shirt and shiny brown boots. He walked a few steps to stand between the two lines. The children stood even straighter, more rigid, like soldiers being reviewed.

"At ease," he tried. No one knew what he meant, so they tensed even more.

"I say," he laughed easily, as he had with the men at Dawson's, "I am glad to meet you all, but you must know this is new to me. The schools I attended were different, so I am not sure what we are supposed to do next. Can some of you help out?"

Maureen looked back at Phoebe. Phoebe took a deep breath.

"You're supposed to ring the big bell, and then tell us to go in," she managed. "Or you could have someone ring it for you if you want."

"Very well, would you please ring the bell?" he asked Gus Pfitzer, who was at the head of the boys' line, "and let's all go inside. I find it a bit chilly here in the wind."

He walked on in. Since he did not seem intent on giving any further orders the children hesitantly followed him. Without watching them, he walked to the front of the room, quickly leafed through the books on the table, scanned those in the bookcase, and whirled the globe. By then the children had all slipped into their seats and were sitting silently with hands folded on their desks.

He looked over the room as he walked to the desk, then back to the side. No one moved. No one even seemed to breathe. Gus, after a good swing on the bell, tried to tiptoe in but stumbled over the cob basket. The children near him hissed, "Sh-h-h!"

Otherwise, all was silent.

The schoolmaster walked back to the desk, opened the ledger and ran his finger down.

"Miss Moore? Miss Maureen Moore?"

He looked up.

Gulping, Maureen answered, "Present."

"Perhaps you could help us get started," he said. He seemed a little nervous.

Maureen ducked her head, and said so low it was hard to hear her. "Phoebe knows better than me."

Phoebe kicked Maureen under the seat they shared, but she tried to keep her feelings from showing on her face.

"Phoebe? Miss Dawson? Could you come up?"

Swallowing past the tight place in her throat, Phoebe obediently walked to the front. In a low voice, just to her, Mr. Gould said, "Thank you. Please advise me—how do we start? And how does one teach so many ages all at once?"

Phoebe thought to herself, "If I were going to start a new job and had four days to get ready, I would at least have found out what to do first."

But he smiled in such a friendly, appealing way she began to forgive him for saying, "if girls could learn anything at all."

"First you read from the Bible, and then we say the Lord's Prayer, and then we sing the 'Star Spangled Banner.'

"Then you give the different ones their lessons. Everyone studies while you hear the different classes recite at the front table. If you want me to, I will set copy for the little ones, while you get the middle ones started."

"Fine. Thank you. Thank you very much."

He smiled again and added softly, "You may be seated if you wish. I will struggle through the first part."

Calmly, as though he had planned to do it all along, Mr. Gould flipped to a place in the Bible and hardly looking at it, read:

> *"But where shall wisdom be found?*
> *And where is the place of understanding?*
> *Man knoweth not the price thereof;*
> *It cannot be gotten for gold,*
> *Neither shall silver be weighed for the price thereof.*
> *It cannot be valued with the gold of Ophir,*
> *With the precious onyx, or the sapphire.*
> *Gold and glass cannot equal it;*
> *Neither shall the exchange thereof be jewels of fine gold,*
> *No mention shall be made of coral or of crystal;*
> *Yea, the price of wisdom is above rubies.*
> *God understandeth the way thereof,*

And unto man he said,
'Behold, the fear of the Lord, that is wisdom;
And to depart from evil is understanding.'"

With the first phrase all the school came to attention.

"He reads like music!" Maureen whispered to Phoebe.

"And who plays the organ?" Mr. Gould asked. Their blank looks answered, and he shrugged.

"No one? Then I shall play while you sing."

Without any apparent thought of paper wads or spit-balls, he turned his back to the school and frowned as he ripped the paper away from the bench, disclosing a lovely tapestry the children had not even known was there. He pushed and pulled at the knobs, pumped a few times, spread his fingers over the keys and music filled the room.

For the first time, they understood what the organ was. His hands, as Hartley said later, were all over the place at once, but his fingers seemed to know their way around. After a few beautiful sounds, up and down, he started the familiar national anthem. He played some of the first, then the last, then started again at the first, singing as he played.

None of them had ever heard anyone sing like that before. They stood entranced, listening. No one thought of peeping. So the teacher sang it through, and when the last rich, clear notes died away, little Abe exclaimed "Oh-h-h" and clapped his hands. Then he hid his head on his desk.

The teacher swung around to face the school. After a pause he announced, "You may be seated."

Quietly they slid into their seats.

Hartley raised his hand. Mr. Gould seemed pleased.

"Yes?" he asked.

"I wondered about your horse. Would you like me to give him some hay and take off the bridle?"

"Oh, of course. Thank you very much, Hartley. He will stand, but I did not intend to leave him like that. I was distracted, I fear."

Hartley had worried about the horse, so he was glad he had finally gotten up the courage to ask. He repeated to himself, "distracted, distracted," so he would not forget it. He did not know what it meant, but he was certainly not going to ask until he got home or had a chance to look it up for himself.

"Some civilized he is!" Hartley muttered to himself and the horse as he unbuckled the bridle and made a halter from an extra rope to tie the horse to the rack before forking down a generous pile of hay. "Doesn't know enough to put up his horse!"

Going home that afternoon the Dawson children and the Moores sang until the worn ridges turned off toward the Moore place. The Dawsons were still singing as they reached their own windmill, where they stopped at the tank to let the horses drink.

Perhaps by chance their mother and father were both there waiting, their mother holding Mary Ann. Martha played with a kitten. The buggy children piled out, the older two slid quickly off their horses, and all began talking at once. Their parents' anxious looks changed to beaming smiles as the happy children interrupted each other's reports.

"Oh, Father, you should hear him play the organ! And sing at the same time!" Phoebe grabbed up Martha and swung her around until Martha giggled.

"And read the Bible. Like Maureen said, he reads like music. It was a wonderful piece—he wrote it down for me." Tessie pulled a piece of paper from her dress. "Job 28:12. He says that whole book is an interesting story. It seemed new."

David added, "He didn't have us recite much at all, Mother, but he told us stories, new stories. There was a slave named E-sup—see, I did remember it, Robbie—and he was not black, but he was a slave, and he told lots of stories, and one was about a fox that wanted some grapes."

"I thought that was silly," Robbie interrupted, "because foxes don't eat grapes, but teacher said lots of folks think they want something that they don't really have any use for."

"Well, that slave told all those stories, and someone wrote them down, and soon as I learn to read, I can read every one of them. Teacher said."

"He told a story—the teacher, I mean—that some blind man wrote. I forget his name, but it was about a soldier named 'Ah-kill-eze' spelled A-c-h-i-l-l-e-s," Hartley reported, "and he was the best fighter in the whole army, but he got mad because he could not have his own way, and he pouted in his tent, and the enemy just about won, and killed Ah-kill-eze's best friend, and then Ah-kill-eze finally started fighting again, and his side won. But it was hard on his friend."

"And there is a lot more in that book, and tomorrow Mr. Gould is going to bring it. Gopher and me, I mean I, and all of us that want to can read it all."

Hartley was removing bridles from the horses, with his father's help, as he talked.

"What about you, Daughter?" Mr. Dawson patted Tessie's hair as she stood quietly smiling into space. "Did you hear stories, too?"

"We all did. When he started to talk, everyone stopped to listen, but he was not cross, he just walked around showing what the people did and making his voice different for everyone in the story. And he sang!"

Phoebe set Martha on the fence. "He taught us some new songs too. Did you hear the one we were singing? It was made up by a real American. His name was John Howard Payne, and he wrote whole plays like Shakespeare and some operas, that's plays with music, and one of the

73

songs was the one he taught us. Come on, Tessie, boys—let's sing it again for the rest of them."

Hartley gave a final slap to the horses, who by now knew that food was waiting in their stalls and went to find it. Hartley joined the others. Standing close together, they hummed softly, watching Phoebe until she gave a little signal with her hand. Then their voices blended together, high and clear as they sang happily:

"Mid pleasures and palaces though I may roam,
Be it ever so humble, there's no place like home."

Mr. Dawson laid his arm across his wife's shoulders as they listened. She reached up to squeeze his hand, and then bowed her head and said, "Thank you, God."

"Amen," their father added.

"And he doesn't get mad at people drawing pictures! He said drawing pictures is something that proves people are different from other animals, like singing and laughing. He said we are all animals, every one of us, but other animals can't sing or draw pictures or learn to read or laugh. But people can, so that is why they go to school."

"And at noon, when little Abe started to tell about rabbits in the hedge and he stuttered and Gus laughed, the teacher picked up Abe and set him on the bell-frame rail, where he could look right at him and said, 'Abe, don't pay any attention to foolish people who don't know when to laugh and when not to. Go slow, look just at me, and tell me about the rabbits.'

"And do you know, Abe hardly stuttered at all!"

"Well, well—you all seem to have a lot to tell. Let's get chores done up, and we will hear more at supper!" Mrs. Dawson said happily.

Day after day, the children were ready early, eager to get to school. Teacher showed anyone who wanted to learn how to play the organ. Hartley, Phoebe, Tessie and David were all eager to get their turns.

"Teacher brought the Achilles book, and some more," Hartley reported one day after school. "Two, named *Little Men* and *Little Women*, were written by a friend of his."

"And guess what, Mother! She is the daughter of Mr. Alcott, the man who wrote that piece about vegetables in the kings' courts in olden times, in the *Appleton Sixth Reader*. Her name is Louisa May Alcott, and if our new baby is a girl, I hope we can name her Louisa May!" Phoebe said excitedly.

One afternoon when David and Robbie came home with mud on their hands, their clothes and in their hair, their mother frowned.

"Have you boys been up to mischief?" she questioned.

"Us? Oh, the mud. No, that's from the maps. You see, the teacher says maps are pictures of countries, and real countries have hills, and high hills called mountains, and trees and flat prairie and creeks and all sorts of stuff. The book pictures don't show them good, so we are making maps outside with mud, and sticking in hedge pieces for trees, and rocks where they are supposed to be and heaps of dirt for mountains, and digging a big hole for the oceans. There's lots of oceans in the world. About ten bucketfuls!" Robbie explained.

One Saturday morning Robbie and David burst into the house calling the girls.

"Come! Come see! Hartley's got a rattlesnake for school!"

Phoebe and Tessie were cleaning the parlor, but they dropped their broom and dustpan, grabbed jackets from the hook by the kitchen door and ran with their brothers toward the lane.

"Children!" their mother called after them in alarm, but they seemed not to hear.

Their father ran from the barn. He found them all gathered in excitement around a small box which did, indeed, contain a lethargic rattlesnake.

"What do you mean, 'It's for school'?" he demanded. "I thought you liked Mr. Gould! But even if you were going to play pranks, you know enough not to do anything danger-ous. A rattlesnake is not a toy, and you know it!"

"It's not for playing, it's for learning," Hartley said indignantly.

"We're having a museum—that's where you collect things—of all the animals that live around here."

"The little ones. Not buffalo, of course."

"We are building a place to keep them in the shed. We are going to have jack rabbits, and prairie dogs if we can catch some. Gopher Martin said for sure he is going to bring a gopher!"

"And we'll have turtles," Tessie added, "and catfish and carp from the creek."

"And my frogs. I am sorry I wasted those on old Mud Turtle, but I'll find some more," Robbie promised.

"And worms," David said. "Mr. Gould said worms are to learn about, too."

"Gus Pfitzer said he could bring a baby skunk, but Mr. Gould said maybe not."

"I should think not!" Mr. Dawson agreed.

"But Gus has been trapping them and selling the skins, and he said he would give a skin all cleaned."

"And Father, do you know Mr. Gould said his teacher in Harvard, Mr. Agassiz, said outdoors is the place to learn about things. By the time someone wrote it in a book, things got mixed up too often, so you should learn to look around you, and look up at the stars, and study things the way they live."

Phoebe leaned over to peek again at the snake.

Tessie announced, with firmness unusual for her, "And Mr. Agassiz' wife says education is very important for women, and they can learn anything boys can, and they ought to, and so does Mr. Alcott. Mr. Gould says he thinks now they are right. I'm going to learn everything about animals and bugs, and I'm going to learn their real names."

"I am, too," Phoebe and Hartley chimed in. Robbie and David echoed them.

Phoebe explained, "The names we call them by are not their real names. They are just English names, sort of like your pet name at home in your own family. The real names are in Latin, so everyone in the world can understand. People in Switzerland and Germany, where Mr. Gould went to school, and where the Pfitzers come from, they know the same Latin names as people in America or England who study them. Everyone knows what everyone else is talking about, and that is handy—don't you think so, Father?

"I remember the name of the meadowlark. The real name is *Sturnella neglecta* and its family name is *Icteridae*."

She laughed. "I'll bet Mother doesn't know we have neighbors named *Icteridae*!"

"And I'll bet you didn't know the name of rattlesnakes is *Crotalus*, and their family name is *Crotalidae*. I'm going to put old *Crutalus'* name on his box," Hartley added.

"What is the Latin name of frogs, Hartley?"

"I don't know, Robbie, but the teacher will—he knows everything," Hartley promised confidently.

Mr. Dawson shook his head, but in spite of the surprise of the news, he agreed that studying the things living around them seemed to be a good idea.

Not all the parents were as easily convinced. But the museum grew, and the children began bringing home papers they had written describing the animals.

"Just like the children did at Plumfield, where Miss Alcott wrote about," Phoebe said.

Tessie was very proud of her report on chickens: "Chickens are animals, too. They are good for eggs and for chicken and dumplings and other things. They make good gravy. Their name is *Gallus Gallus*. The Greek people had them. So did the Roman people. So do we. We have Rhode Island Reds. They are named for the state of Rhode Island because they used to live there and I guess some still do but ours live in Kansas. They eat wheat and worms and grasshoppers. The mother scratches in the dirt and calls her babies to come eat. But all the rooster does is crow every morning when it gets light. Roosters are good baked or boiled but they don't lay eggs."

Mr. and Mrs. Dawson laughed when she read it to them.

"That is a fine report, Daughter, and we are proud of you. Perhaps soon we can have a literary society in the neighborhood, and you can read your reports there."

The children announced that as soon as everyone got to school the next day, they were all going to visit *Cynomus Ludo vicianuss*, in their town several miles west. "That's prairie dogs, Mother," Phoebe explained. Many of the children had been there, but not all, and when they told Mr. Gould about the many little hills the prairie dogs built, with tunnels they could jump down into, Mr. Gould asked how high the hills were, and how wide, and no one knew for sure. So he said they would all go visit, and learn more about such interesting neighbors.

Mrs. Dawson shook her head at her husband.

"Some of the patrons are going to complain, Francis. I know they are. They will think that if they are paying a man to teach school, he should keep the children in school and make them do lessons."

"Of course, some will complain," he replied. "The less most people know, the more they think they know about how to teach school. But I think it is a good idea. Don't you?"

"I think it is splendid. I think Mr. Gould is right that children learn more from watching and writing books than they do from only reading. And it whets their appetites to read more. At least it has for our children. But some won't like it."

"I'll tell you what, Marian. Let's take the wagon and go along. We might send Hartley over to see if Ellen Moore and her young ones would like the outing. Then if there are complaints, I will know first hand what was going on. I think I'd like to watch that young man in action."

And so it was that when the children gathered at school the next morning, bubbling with excitement, they quickly slid into places, talking softly to each other until the first note of the organ rang out. They were intent on the teacher, paying no attention to the grownups in the back. The teacher played softly for a few minutes. Then he read from the Bible, *"The earth is the Lord's and the fullness thereof, the world, and they that dwell therein."*

Together they bowed their heads and said the "Our Father" a little hastily. The teacher turned to the organ again, and on the first chord all sprang up. After some more notes, he raised one hand toward them. They sang, with all their hearts and voices, "Oh, say, can you see, by the dawn's early light ..."

After the first few words Mr. and Mrs. Dawson, and then Mrs. Moore, joined in, until the schoolhouse seemed to be bursting with music.

The teacher announced then, "Everyone mounted and ready. Stay together. Hartley will lead the way, as we planned, and the wagons will follow. Gopher and Gus will be the rear guard."

Out again they all dashed, racing to be first in wagons or buggies, or onto riding horses. They wheeled into place and on Hartley's signal set off across the wide-stretching brown fields, with Hartley proudly prancing in front on Pal. Phoebe stayed beside Maureen and her wagonload of little brothers and sisters, with Martha joining them. Kathleen was along, too, while Mrs. Moore and her baby rode with the Dawsons. Before they crossed the creek at the ford, Hartley pulled up and advised, "After we get past the creek and out into the prairie grass, we'd better stop singing and talking and be as quiet as we can or we won't see any."

They were rather shouted out by then, anyway, so they played they were Indians sneaking up on settlers, and managed to be fairly quiet. They stopped the wagons a distance from the mounds, tied the horses, and on foot went closer.

Despite the children's precautions, the little furry animals, sitting erect on top of their mounds, darted down out of sight. By the time the last children arrived there was only a series of dirt piles.

Mr. Gould gave out pieces of string, and told the children, "Measure how long a string it takes from the top of a mound to the ground level, and make a knot there. Then see how much string across, and make two knots in that one, so you don't mix them up. Then bring your strings back and measure them on this marked tape, and we will write down the figures."

The younger ones worked with some of the older children. When they had their figures on the paper, Mr. Gould supervised Hartley, Gus and Phoebe. They added the inches everyone had gotten for the height, and then divided it by the number of groups that had measured a mound. They did the same for the width.

"That is called 'the average'; the biggest and the littlest sort of balance each other, and you can find out how big most of the mounds are," Mr. Gould explained.

"The average size is eighteen inches high and five feet, six inches across," he finally announced.

Mr. Gould suggested, "Perhaps if we sit down and keep very still, some of them will get brave and come up again. Here are field glasses—you can take turns looking through them."

Tired, the children waited and watched. Sure enough one adventurous head soon popped up, looked around, and, sensing no danger, climbed on top.

"Ooooh! There's one!" Irene exclaimed as a furry head disappeared.

"Aw, you scared him. Can't you keep still?" Sean scolded his little sister. She ran to hide her head against her mother, and again the children waited quietly. Again a head came up, and slowly the mounds, one by one, were occupied.

Quietly Mr. Gould passed around pieces of paper with pencils fastened to pieces of cardboard.

"Try to draw them," he whispered. "Or draw their homes—whatever you see. Remember, look carefully."

Irene took her paper back to her mother; she made a few lines, but then Irene became interested in something a few of the other smaller children were doing back at the wagon and ran off.

Her mother, looking after her, suddenly smiled. She began drawing steadily, looking back and forth from the prairie dogs to her paper.

Sitting beside her, Mrs. Dawson looked on curiously. Then she smiled and motioned to her husband, who quietly moved in behind. He looked surprised and smiled.

Mrs. Moore did not seem to notice them. She continued to look at the prairie dogs, some appearing, some ducking into their holes. Now and again one ventured down a little ways into a clearing between the mounds.

The quiet could not last long. Children began taking their papers to Mr. Gould, who nodded approval at each one, and said, "That's fine! Very good!"

But when they had all finished and began playing tag, or eating lunch, Mrs. Moore was still drawing, although the new commotion had driven all the prairie dogs back into their tunnels.

Mr. Gould brought the children's drawings over to show the three parents. He was smiling proudly.

"Look at this—real perspective—and here is a remarkably accurate one," he said.

Mr. Dawson agreed, and then said, "And see what we have here," he pointed to Mrs. Moore, who had at last finished. She was holding her paper up, inspecting it with her head tucked to one side. Only then did she notice the attention she was getting, and that her daughters and Phoebe, Hartley and Gopher were laughing where they had gathered. She started to turn the paper face down on her lap, but Mr. Gould and Kathleen both reached for it.

"Let the teacher see it, Mother," Kathleen urged. "Isn't she good, Teacher?"

Mr. Gould took the paper. And then he laughed. Mrs. Moore had captured the motions of the curious little animals, some on top of their mounds, some peeking over, some alert a few inches away. But on each prairie dog she had drawn a very human face, all of which resembled members of the school. The one in the center, facing the world with a quizzical expression was without a doubt her own son Sean.

"Excellent! Excellent!" the teacher exclaimed.

Mrs. Dawson said, "I didn't dream you could draw like that, Ellen. I don't see how you do it!"

Mrs. Moore, her voice strange, watched the paper as it was passed carefully around the admiring group.

"In the auld country I loved to draw," she said dreamily. "My father carved stone and wood for the churches and the big houses of the gentry. His father before him had been a stone carver too. When I was a small girl yet, I drew pictures for them to work from. But I've not had a pencil in my hand these many, many months. Here there are so many things for a body to be doing. But thank you, schoolmaster, for teaching the little ones to look about them. My grandfather always urged, 'It's the lookin' that is important.' And I guess it's a lesson I've been forgettin'. I was after thinkin' here there was nothing to draw. I was indeed forgettin' to look about me."

Kathleen and Maureen hugged their mother, and Mr. Gould, with the paper again in his hands, said, "You have a talent, Mrs. Moore. You must teach the others."

At home that evening, when the Dawsons were reviewing the gala day as they ate their supper, Phoebe remarked thoughtfully, "Isn't it interesting? We went out to learn to look at our neighbors *Cynomus Ludovicianus*—and the most important thing we learned was about our neighbor Ellen Moore."

SOD SCHOOLHOUSE

CHAPTER FIVE

A Permanent Replacement

TESSIE SAT CROSS-LEGGED on the buffalo robe in front of the open stove in the dining room. One tear after another rolled down her face and dropped dismally from her chin onto the mass of dark red yarn in her lap. Her knitting needles swiftly slid in and out by touch alone; her vision, blurred by her tears, did not slow her progress.

It was beautiful yarn. Old Mrs. Osborn had given it to her for helping with cooking and dishes during the old woman's "spell" with rheumatism. Mr. Osborn had sheared it from his own sheep. His wife had carded and spun it herself and dyed it with mulberry juice. Tessie had been thrilled to get the treasure and started at once to knit a muffler for Mr. Gould's Christmas present.

And now he was gone!

Someone Back East had died. His family had sent for him and his sudden absence left a great emptiness behind. All the children mourned, but Tessie could not be comforted. She would not listen to talk about letters from possible new teachers.

"I don't want a new teacher," was all she would say.

"No one wants a new teacher instead of him, but we can't have him, so what's the use of crying about it?" Phoebe demanded as she ran the skimmer around a milk crock to take off the cream.

"Phoebe!" her mother cautioned, "you're getting milk into the cream!"

"Well, just when everything is going splendidly, everything goes wrong," Phoebe muttered.

"Not everything, really, Daughter. We knew all along he could not stay. Let's be thankful for what God has given. You can never lose the experience of the past weeks, and some people never have such riches."

"Yes, Mother."

Phoebe gave a last flip, covered the crock, and added the cream to the cream crock. She poured boiling water from the simmering teakettle into the stone churn, swished it around, emptied it, and scalded the wooden dasher. She dumped the crockful of cream in so hard it slopped over a little. Phoebe cleaned out the crock with her finger, licking it while her mother looked the other way, and set the crock on the table to be washed. Pulling the kitchen stool over with one foot, she sat down and began slamming the dasher down and down again.

"Phoebe!" her mother exclaimed, "You won't help anything by cracking the bottom of the churn. Either do it right, or leave it."

"I'm sorry," she said, swinging into a more gentle churning rhythm.

Outside there was a scritch of crackling snow followed by the stomping of boots and the voices of Hartley and their father. They left their snowy overshoes on the covered porch, stepped into house slippers waiting on the shelf inside the door and bustled in quickly, pushing the door against the icy wind.

"How is the weather?" Mrs. Dawson asked.

"Cold but clearing, and the sun is bright. It will be a good trip. Did you tell Phoebe?"

"Tell me what?"

"We're going!" Hartley rubbed his hands above the stove, dumping in more cobs for a quick, hotter fire.

"Going where?"

"To Wichita! With Father, Mr. Martin and Mr. Pfitzer to meet the new teacher."

"To Wichita!" Phoebe stopped churning and turned to look at her father in disbelief.

"That is, if you want to," he teased. "Gopher was just here. We are going early in the morning in their new sleigh. The teacher wanted to meet some of the scholars as well as the board members, so we decided to take you two and Gus and Gopher. It will be a tight squeeze, but we will be warmer."

"Is she really coming, then?"

"She is coming from Lawrence to Wichita on the train. She has relatives near there. We will meet her at the hotel. We did not want to take another teacher sight unseen, even on Professor Carroll's recommendation. Remember him, Phoebe? He wrote that she was an excellent student at the university, and she taught before she came. He thinks she will be very competent. But 'once burned, fire-shy,' and it seems she feels the same way. After we all talk things over, if we are satisfied and she is, too, she will visit there a few days and her relatives will bring her over. If not, she will go back to Lawrence."

Hartley could barely contain himself.

"And we will see Wichita! And the trains! And the cattle coming from Texas! And stay overnight in a hotel!"

Phoebe found it hard to take it all in. Slowly churning again, she began thinking of trains—those huge, roaring monsters like dragons in stories. She had seen them steaming and grinding and snorting along their iron ribbons from out of the distance to come to a noisy stop in Newton. And the cattle on the Chisholm Trail, and stores, and staying at a hotel!

But most of all she wondered what the new teacher would be like. The rest of the surprise would have been almost too much excitement to bear if not for the worry about the teacher. A woman teacher!

"Don't worry about the new teacher," Hartley said, "If she comes, we can handle her!"

Pat Moore and Maureen came over to help Mrs. Dawson with the chores. The sleigh pulled up long before sunrise. Mrs. Dawson supervised packing the travelers in with buffalo robes and wool comforts, with hot stones at their feet and hot baked potatoes to hold in their hands and later eat for a snack.

Bells on the harnesses kept time to the hoofbeats, muffled by the snow. The slender sleigh runners skimmed easily over the crust, and yet, with no close object to gauge movement by, they seemed to stay forever in the same spot in the vast, stretching white. Snuggled in front between her father and Mr. Martin, Phoebe soon grew sleepy. She spent most of the trip in a drowsy blur until Mr. Pfitzer pulled to a stop.

"Are we in Wichita?" she cried out, coming to with a jerk.

Everyone laughed.

"I reckon not. We are about halfway to the Mastersons'," her father explained. "We will bait the horses here and feed ourselves, too. This used to be a stage stop before the railroad came through; the folks still have quite a few travelers stop, homesteaders and such on their way through. We'll all have some hot coffee and get our stones hot again. How are your toes?"

"Just fine. When do you think we will get to the Mastersons'?"

"In plenty of time for Catherine to get up a good dinner for us all. You and Hartley can renew acquaintances with the children. Catherine will want to know all the news of your mother, and what we have heard from Illinois. Maybe she hasn't heard the Mullins are planning to homestead here this spring—don't forget to tell her. I'll probably be busy with Thomas."

The Mastersons had lived near Mrs. Dawson's family Back East. When they moved to Kansas, three years before, they had naturally stayed a few days with the Dawsons to break their long trip. Phoebe remembered how her mother had enjoyed hearing news of old friends and relatives that she had not seen for so many years. And Phoebe remembered how the seven Masterson children and she and Hartley and Tessie had played tag and told riddles.

Minnie Masterson, the youngest, was about Hartley's age, and the others were stairsteps up to the big grown-up brothers, Ed, Jim and Bat. They knew lots of good songs. In the evening both families sat around a campfire outdoors, because they could not all crowd into the old soddy, and sang. The women talked about home and the men talked about the government. It would be fun to see them again. Plans were to stop there for a good visit, warm up before dinner, and give the horses a rest. Then they would be halfway to Wichita, and should reach their hotel well before dark.

The Mastersons were indeed surprised but delighted at the unexpected visitors. Nellie, now eighteen, at once set seventeen-year-old Tom to ringing chicken necks while she began rolling out piecrust. Minnie and Phoebe began peeling a huge vat of potatoes and of turnips, while fifteen-year-old George took Hartley, Gopher and Gus to the barn to help rub down the horses, water them and blanket them against the cold.

"I wish you could stay longer," Minnie told Phoebe. "The big boys, Ed and Bat, have been out West at Dodge City, and you'd love to hear some of the stories they tell."

When the girls had finished their chore, Minnie took Phoebe to the loft where she slept to bring out a scrapbook with a clipping from the *Wichita Eagle* dated April 30, 1874. It was about the wedding of a friend of Ed's, Henry Raymond, and a schoolteacher, Ida Curtiss. The paper said it was the first wedding in Grant Township. It told who was there and who was the preacher—no one Phoebe had ever heard of. But Minnie, giggling, pointed to the bottom and read: "...among others present at the wedding in the morning and the party in the evening were—the fair belle of Sunnydale,

Miss Nellie Masterson, and her charming sister Minnie ... the genial Dr. Ed. Masterson; that old buffalo slayer, 'Cheyenne Jim' Masterson ..."

It was pretty exciting, Phoebe thought, to have a friend who had had her name in the *Wichita Eagle* and been called charming.

As the rested horses skimmed on toward Wichita at a steady pace, Mr. Dawson told the others about the two older Masterson boys.

"Ed and Bat, back in '72, shortly after they came out from Illinois, sub-contracted to build a spur railroad for the Santa Fe from Fort Dodge out to the new Dodge City. A man named Ritter, the main contractor, refused to pay them—I guess he thought he could get away with it because they were so young. Ed was about twenty, then, and Bat nineteen. Bat cornered the man at gunpoint, took the money he had on him and counted out what was due to Ed and him. He gave the rest back, and the boys went their way."

Mr. Martin shook his head.

"The characters pouring into these new cow towns grow up fast from driving all those cattle up from Texas. In such a new town, with people looking for excitement or to skin someone looking for excitement, it is going to take some doing to get any respect for law and order."

Mr. Pfitzer said, "I got relatives at Newton. Newton is not so wild, now that the big drives load at Wichita. But with all the killings there's been in Wichita I am glad the team makes good time. We'll get there safe inside before dark."

Mr. Martin said, "I hear they got a purty good marshal in Wichita now, that Meagher, and his policeman, Earp. They don't let much get by. But they got a lot of trouble. I hope my boys don't go to be marshals."

"Father," Hartley asked, "George said Bat signed on as an Indian Scout last year, and he got seventy-five dollars a month. Do you believe it?"

"It's true son."

"How much did you say you have raised to pay the new schoolteacher?"

"Twenty-five dollars a month."

"And she's been to college, and everything?"

"Yes, she has been to college."

"Huh!"

The miles passed quickly, and soon there was the big sign telling them they had arrived: "Wichita–Anything goes. Leave your guns with the marshal and get a receipt."

They had no guns, so they went on, driving slowly now to take in the sights. They passed the Harris House, where the owner, a Mr. Ledford, had been shot four years before by a U.S. marshal and a scout. The incident became infamous because it was the first time there had been bloodshed in the streets of the then year-old town.

They made their way among farm wagons, prairie schooners, Texans in big hats and spurs riding horseback, Mexicans, women alone in elegant clothes, women in ordinary clothes in groups with children holding their skirts. At the corner of Douglas and Main, where they were admiring the big New York Store that Mr. Dawson promised they would all go inside the next day and do some shopping for gifts, an express wagon pounded pell-mell down the street, scattering frightened horses and people on foot and barely missing an ox-drawn prairie schooner.

It was getting to be too much excitement for one day. Mr. Pfitzer slapped the reins and Mr. Dawson directed him to the side-street hotel where they were to stay.

Although from May to September the town was jammed with people—cowboys who brought the thousands of cattle from Texas to ship from Wichita on the new railroad and people from all over the country who came to make money from the cowboys when they were paid off—now, in the early winter, there were few outsiders. Mr. Dawson was assured there was plenty of room for his party.

A man behind a long counter in what looked to Phoebe like an unusually big parlor asked Mr. Dawson to sign a big ledger. Then, reading the names, he said, "Mr. Dawson and party? Miss Jorgensdatter is expecting you. She is in the private parlor, if you will please follow me."

"Jorgensdatter—that's a funny name," Phoebe remarked as they followed the man down a narrow carpeted hall.

"It is Scandinavian," her father explained. "Datter means daughter—her whole name means Jorgen's daughter. It really is not any funnier than our name, Dawson—not as funny, really, as calling a girl Daw's son."

The man knocked on the door. A woman's voice answered, clear and somehow special. As they went in she was sitting, erect and graceful, at the table at the far end of the room, writing with a steel pen. She rose gracefully, and with a smooth long stride crossed the room and held out her hand to Mr. Dawson as a man might have. Phoebe was entranced.

Phoebe had hardly gotten her breath when she heard her father pronouncing her name. The woman then turned to her, again holding out her hand and repeating, "Phoebe Dawson. I am happy to meet you."

Her eyes met Phoebe's in a way that ever after seemed to be what she remembered most about Miss Jorgensdatter. She really looked at people, and she listened to them. She smiled a warm, calm smile, then in turn shook hands with each of the others.

"Won't you all sit down? I am sure you are tired and cold after your long ride. I asked the hotel people to bring some coffee and rolls to warm you until dinner is served."

"She must mean supper," Gus whispered. "Noon is gone a long time ago, and we had dinner."

The boys crowded together onto a long sofa against the back wall. Mr. Dawson motioned Phoebe, as though she were a grownup, into one of the red plush chairs. He and the other men waited until the woman had seated herself again before they sank rather heavily into black leather-covered chairs with balls for feet. Phoebe was trying not to stare. She remembered that it was rude, but she could not easily keep her eyes from what seemed like a living picture.

As the woman shifted slightly to face Mr. Dawson, Phoebe could watch without feeling noticed. The late afternoon sunshine through the window fell directly on the woman. The skin on her face and hands was the whitest Phoebe had ever seen. They really looked like snow, which had always seemed such a silly comparison in poems.

Her hair was between yellow and red, in smooth, thick braids wound around her head in a heavy crown, with little wisps of curls pulling out around her face. Her thin lips were bright red, not brownish-red at all. Her mouth and chin were large and square, not exactly pretty but hard not to watch. When she smiled she revealed large, square white even teeth. Her neck was long and white, framed in a greenish-blue jacket over a white shirtwaist. Her skirt, which matched her jacket, was fitted at the waist and flared to her ankles. It rippled when she walked, falling smoothly from a medium-sized bustle.

Her eyes were the same greenish-blue as her dress, and they crinkled when she smiled. As she talked, she held her hands folded firmly in her lap. Her voice was low, but as penetrating as her eyes. Phoebe thought, "I'll bet she could be heard in the back of the school without ever yelling at all."

Mr. Dawson told briefly of the history of the school, and when he uneasily confessed that the boys had buried the schoolmaster in the mud, the woman laughed, a rollicking, gay laugh.

"I've heard of many kinds of student rebellion," she said, "but never any that seemed so like poetic justice."

The men relaxed some after that. Phoebe knew they had been uneasy about whether she would want to undertake a school where such a thing had happened, but she seemed undisturbed.

"We know that keeping discipline is a big problem in many schools," Mr. Dawson said. "The school district north of ours, some eight years old, has had constant trouble. We want to have a school the children will respect, and where they will learn what they are supposed to, instead of bad habits."

The other men nodded their heads vigorously. Mr. Dawson glanced at them, and both nodded at him. Already they had decided. Mr. Dawson went on.

"I speak for the whole board when I say that if you see fit to undertake the school, we will help with the discipline. Mr. Gould did not want to attempt the big boys, since he was not really prepared as a teacher. But the boys' families understandably want equal opportunities for all the children. Those boys—young men, really—perhaps need school most of all.

"Of course, we would not expect a young woman to deal with young men almost as old as she is," he smiled. Phoebe noticed that Miss Jorgensdatter did not smile, but continued to listen earnestly, waiting.

Mr. Dawson, after a pause that showed his surprise, continued, "Professor Carroll writes that you are an excellent scholar yourself, and that you have taught before, which," he bowed slightly, "I can well believe. Our suggestion is, that if you are willing to take the school, one of us from the school board, or one of the other patrons, will take turns staying at the school to keep order, and give you a free hand to instruct.

Our children already are far behind. But if we could have a successful four-month term, they could all get a solid beginning. When spring work gets heavy and the older scholars have to help farm, you could continue another month at least with the little ones. So ... we ... we hope you will come," he finished uncertainly as she continued to listen intently without answering.

Now, instead of replying to him directly, she turned suddenly to Phoebe.

"And you, Phoebe Dawson, what do you think of the school?"

Startled, Phoebe tried to look away, but was held by those keen, slightly smiling green eyes looking right at her. Something in her throat kept her voice from coming at first, but she swallowed and was surprised to hear herself say, with growing confidence, "It, it was wonderful when Mr. Gould was there. Maybe we did not do our lessons the way a real teacher would have us, but we learned a lot and it was fun. Most everyone would be good most of the time I think."

When it was clear that Phoebe had stopped, the woman nodded her head slightly with the same calm, warm smile, and startled the boys with the same question.

"And you, Hartley Dawson. What do you think?"

Hartley gulped and said, "Same as Phoebe."

"And you, Edward Martin?"

Gopher seemed to choke and scrubbed his boots in the carpet. At least, Phoebe thought proudly, Hartley had not wiggled like that. The woman waited, relaxed and still, with a pleasant, inquiring look.

Finally Gopher murmured, "Me, too."

"And you, Gustave Pfitzer?"

Quickly Gus said, "Me, too."

Miss Jorgensdatter sat perfectly silent, and Phoebe thought how seldom anyone did that. The woman looked at each of them again, seeming to be thinking. Then she slid back a little in her chair, unfolded her hands and grasped the chair arms firmly.

"It sounds like an interesting opportunity. Gentlemen I will accept. But with this understanding. I appreciate your offer of help. But if I am to be the teacher, I will be in charge. I think the scholars and I will get acquainted better if we work it out ourselves."

The men frowned and looked worried. Before one of them said anything, she went on, "A school is like a little world, and I think it better not to have outsiders present except as visitors. Of course, all eligible scholars in the district will be expected to attend, to behave and to work. But I must do it my own way. If that is agreeable with you, then we will consider it arranged."

The men silently consulted each other. Mr. Dawson glanced at Phoebe, who nodded enthusiastically. Finally he said, "I hope you understand that most of these scholars have never been to school before. Even the younger ones have much to learn about how to act away from home. And I am afraid the young men who have been excluded this past month have not improved. There is reason to believe that they have gotten the idea that school is sort of a duel between teachers and scholars. The neighbors at Texas School have bragged about what rough treatment they have given several teachers, and there are rumors that several of our fellows have plans to compete with Texas."

Miss Jorgensdatter did not look worried, or doubtful. She laughed.

"I understand, Mr. Dawson. I thank you for your honesty, and I understand. You know, I am a frontier girl myself. When I was growing up near Holton we had some fairly rough neighbors in our school."

"Miss Jorgensdatter," Mr. Pfitzer spoke for the first time. In his nervousness his English was more German than usual, "You can't lick dose pig poys und dey shust learn do young ones to be up to tricks."

Phoebe cringed, especially as he said "learn them." She already wanted to make a good impression on the beautiful teacher. But Miss Jorgensdatter had turned to Mr. Pfitzer to listen with the same intense look. Then she smiled.

"Sprechen sie Deutsch?" she asked. Phoebe had learned that from Mrs. Pfitzer. It meant, "Do you speak German?"

Mr. Pfitzer's face lit up as he answered in his own language, and for a few minutes they talked rapidly in German. The teacher turned again to Mr. Dawson.

"I was telling Mr. Pfitzer I have my own ideas of ways to keep order. I studied in Concord, Massachusetts, at the summer school of Mr. Bronson Alcott. I observed some of the schools that were run as he advised. What I have tried of his methods seem better to me than the lickin' and larnin' pattern some people think is the only way. I must insist. If you want me to try your school, it is to be with freedom to use my own methods. If I cannot handle it satisfactorily, then I will resign and you can try a different way."

Phoebe held her breath, hoping her father would choose the right answer. He was again signaling with the other men. This time Mr. Pfitzer smiled and nodded vigorously, and Mr. Martin agreed.

It was settled; Miss Kirsten Jorgensdatter was their new teacher!

Miss Jorgensdatter and the men talked some more about crops, and last year's grasshoppers and possible dangers this year from the eggs that were left; they talked of the railroads' growth and what it would mean to Kansas when the Pacific Railroad finally reached the Pacific Ocean; they discussed the new wheat the Mennonites around Newton were planting, wheat they had brought from Europe and planted in the fall. She said it was harder grained and that someone needed to improve the milling machinery, but the wheat made a good crop. She sounded as though she knew what she was talking about.

She laughed and said of the things the Mennonites had brought, her favorite was a new vine that grew melons like cucumbers but larger, with hard green rinds and bright red insides that were laced with black seeds and wonderfully sweet and juicy. These "watermelons" were eaten raw, like fruit. Mr. Pfitzer had tasted one, and the others said they would like to try. Fruit was the scarcest food on the prairie.

In the hotel dining room, with women serving their plates, they all ate a welcome meal of roast beef and mashed potatoes, fried cabbage, dried peas in cream sauce and buttered turnips. The tablecloth was white and shiny, the knives and forks and spoons were shiny silver. They were all of the same pattern, and the plates had gold borders. The white napkins were big and stiff. Phoebe worried about spilling something, yet so many things had happened she could not worry much about anything. The boys sat together and quietly stuffed food into themselves. The men and Miss Jorgensdatter continued to talk. The women took away the used plates and silver and brought thick apple pie and chocolate cake with chocolate frosting. Phoebe watched carefully the way the women took dirty dishes away from one side and put clean ones and the desserts on from the other side.

Suddenly Miss Jorgensdatter asked, "And what are you thinking of so quietly, Miss Phoebe Dawson?"

Meeting those intense eyes once again, Phoebe felt strangely acquainted. She answered honestly, "I was wondering if you are German and whether you can play the organ."

The woman laughed, such a cheery, enjoyable sort of laugh.

"Yes, I can play the organ a little—enough to sing with. I can play the violin better. Perhaps someone else—you, for instance—can soon play the organ, and then we can have both instruments. For your other question, I speak German a little because my German grandmother lived with us. But I am only part German. I am also part Dane, part Swede, and part Norwegian. With four grandparents who immigrated from four different countries, I am really American hash!"

Phoebe and the men laughed with her.

Phoebe said, "I never thought of it that way, but I guess that is what our school is too—American hash."

Sod Schoolhouse

CHAPTER SIX

STARTING OVER

*T*HE DAWSON CHILDREN once again started early for a first day of school. Hartley was supposed to make the fire, and the others were too excited to stay behind. But this time they found others there early too. The Moore boys, joking that they did not want to miss any time with a pretty teacher, turned their wagon into the schoolyard just in front of the Dawsons. The Lancey team was already tied to the rack, with the little boys beside Wade and Bart, who were standing together at the tailgate.

The big surprises were a strange new buggy and neat bay mare tied at the end of the rack and smoke already curling from the schoolhouse chimney.

"You make the fire?" Hartley asked the Lanceys.

"Nope. Already smokin' when we come."

"It must be the teacher! She must have made it herself!"

"Looks like."

"Why'd we come so early, Wade?" Jim asked. "It's not even time for first bell."

Abe added, "It's c-c-cold s-s-standin' out here!"

Just then the door opened, and Miss Jorgensdatter, in a dark red dress, greeted them.

"Phoebe Dawson, and Hartley and all of you. Come in so we can get acquainted."

In spite of the cold, she waited in the door. Phoebe, already acquainted, led Tessie in. The Moore girls followed.

"Phoebe Dawson, how good to see you again." The teacher's green eyes sparkled as she spoke, as if she were really sincere in her welcome. She shook Phoebe's hand and then shook hands with each of the girls as Phoebe said their names.

The boys started to enter then pulled back into a bunch—some retreated. But the teacher went to them, her hand outstretched.

"Hartley Dawson. I'm glad to see you again. And will you introduce your friends?"

They were in for it. Embarrassed, Hartley muttered each name in a low voice, but she already seemed to know each one. She reached for hands that had not been offered, shaking each one briskly with the same calm, welcoming smile.

"Sean Moore," she repeated each name, more clearly than Hartley had said them. "Pat Moore, Mike Moore, Wade Lancey, Bart Lancey, Jim Lancey, Abe Lancey, Robbie Dawson, David Dawson. I am glad to meet you all. I am Miss Jorgensdatter."

The big boys muttered something unintelligible, ducked their heads and allowed their hands to be shook before sliding into their seats. The little boys looked and melted. The door opened again.

"Edward Martin—good morning. Edward, I understand your friends call you 'Gopher'?" Miss Jorgensdatter inquired.

"Yes'm," he nodded.

"Which do you prefer, Edward or Gopher?"

He grinned. "Gopher seems more like my real name."

"Then Gopher it is."

She turned to the children, who stood uncertainly around the stove. "Aren't you all going to get too warm with your wraps on?" she asked.

The others looked at Phoebe who said, "We thought maybe we were to go back out and get in line. We just came in because you said to get acquainted."

"I see. But I think standing in line is a waste of time and rather silly, don't you? Suppose you all just hang up your things and find your places as the young men have."

The boys looked at each other, shrugged, and rose to remove jackets and caps, hanging them on the hooks at the back, with mittens and scarves stuffed into pockets. Soon they were back in their seats.

Scholars kept arriving—most of the old ones, three of the new Sturgeon family, and four Dienstetters who had not come before because the boys were needed in the fields and their father did not believe in school for girls. But he had become convinced that Kansas expected all citizens to be educated, and girls were citizens, whether he liked it or not. So Helga and Hildegarde, shy and nervous, followed Kurt and Alfred into the room. They smiled timidly at the teacher's greeting, and slid into seats with Phoebe and Tessie, whom they already knew.

Since the teacher said nothing about being quiet, the children began to chatter more noisily. Bart and Wade whispered to each other with sly grins; Hartley, Gus and Gopher busily brought in more coal and cobs; Pat and Mike joined Wade and Bart. Suddenly one of them laughed loudly. The teacher turned from the books she was arranging in piles, and moved quickly toward the four.

The whole room hushed with expectation. Phoebe, who had been combing Tessie's hair, waited with the comb in mid-air. Stopping directly in front of Wade, the teacher looked him right in the eyes and smiled.

"Mr. Wade Lancey," her voice was low, yet it carried through the room, "you seem to be the senior member of the school. May I ask you to ring the first bell? It will need to be loud, and ring it quite a while, because some families might not have been sure whether there is any school today."

She turned to Pat. "And Mr. Patrick Moore, would you please fill the water bucket before we start?"

As though there were no question but that they would do as she asked, she moved over to the little cluster of Dienstetters, asking them to come with her to get their names on the book. Wade and Pat, with some shoving from their brothers, pulled themselves out of their seats. Soon the bell pealed loud and clear, calling across the prairies.

She asked, again her voice soft but clear, "Oh, and Mr. Mike Moore, and Mr. Bart Lancey—do you think the organ is too heavy for you to move? I would like to have it sideways to the room, so you can watch my direction as I play."

"And so she can watch us," Maureen said, grinning at Phoebe.

"Naw, it's not too heavy," the boys agreed. They were busy moving it when the others returned.

The teacher announced, again in tones that carried over the other sounds yet seemed like soft music, "When you are all ready, will you choose your seats, please."

After a few restless motions and uncertain whisperings, soon all the scholars, big and little, were seated. When the room was quiet she spoke.

"I am glad to see so many of you here early and ready for work. My name is Miss Kirsten Jorgensdatter. You may want to know something about me. I was born and grew up in the country near Holton, and I went to a school much like this one, but not quite so large or so nice. I went to the Teachers' Normal School at Emporia, taught near my home, went to the state university at Lawrence, and for a few months to Mr. Alcott's College of Philosophy in Concord, Massachusetts.

"When I was in school we had some good years and some that were not so good. I understand that already here you too have had some good experiences and some that were not so good."

She smiled broadly, and there were a few giggles. "With everyone helping, I think together we can make the rest of this year a time we will all be happy to remember.

"Naturally, you want to know what to expect and what I expect from you. First of all, I assume that all of you are young ladies and gentlemen, and we should not need many rules to get along well together. I want to tell you how delighted I am that the school board seems to have made a mistake. They thought some of the scholars in this school might be less than gentlemen. I am glad to see that the rowdies who were so childish have decided they were too young for school—or perhaps their mammas kept them home."

Someone snickered. The voice stopped instantly and the green-blue eyes, wide and questioning, focused on the back corner. A silent, expectant hush fell on the room.

"I'm sorry—I didn't hear what you said Mr. Moore. Mr. Lancey? Did you have something to say?"

Phoebe and Maureen looked sideways, to see Wade looking away from the intent eyes and blushing dark red. The silence waited. Then he mumbled, "Who, me? No, ma'am, I didn't say anything."

"Pardon me. I should have known that a man your age would be more courteous than to interrupt."

Eyes looked at her sharply, suspecting sarcasm. But she smiled with all innocent friendliness. Wade frowned at his fists, folded on the desk. Bart shifted uneasily and looked around. He shoved the spitballs deeper into his overalls pocket and sat up a little straighter. The teacher continued.

"Because Christmas is so near, I suggest that we change the usual order of the beginning of a term and plan first for our Christmas program. Then you can work on your parts when you have finished your lessons. Just think! When all of you have graduated and your children or maybe your grandchildren are going here, they will look back to this as the first Christmas of the Freedom School District. There will never be another first one, so it seems to me we should try to make it superb. Don't you think so?"

Practically no one knew what "superb" meant—but it sounded good the way she said it. Without thinking, they chorused "Yes!"

"Splendid."

She began the Bible reading. It was crisp and clear, not musical, like Mr. Gould's, but businesslike information she found interesting and wanted to share with friends:

> "He that handleth a matter wisely shall find good.
> Understanding is a wellspring of life unto him
> that hath it; but the instruction of fools is folly.
> The heart of the wise teacheth his mouth,
> and addeth learning to his lips.
> Pleasant words are as an honeycomb,
> sweet to the soul and health to the bones.
> An ungodly man diggeth up evil; and in
> his lips there is as a burning fire.
> A forward man soweth strife; and a
> whisperer separateth chief friends.
> A violent man enticeth his neighbor, and
> leadeth him into the way that is not good.
> He shutteth his eyes to devise forward things,
> moving his lips he bringeth evil to pass.
> He that is slow to anger is better than the mighty and
> he that ruleth his spirit than he that taketh a city."

When they had finished the prayer, and the teacher was opening the organ, Maureen whispered, "You sure can tell a lot about a person by what they find in the holy word, can't you now?" Phoebe agreed.

The teacher did not play as beautifully as Mr. Gould, but she set a fast, steady pace and hit the low notes hard to keep everyone in time. While her hands played, her eyes watched everyone in the room. She sang and smiled, and the ones who had sung with Mr. Gould followed happily, singing with breath in their lungs as he had taught them. The others made no trouble.

After the opening exercises were finished, she quickly handed out piles of papers to several of the front-row children and asked them to pass them on.

"We will have our singing lesson together before we divide into classes," she explained. "Here are the words to "America" and to a beautiful Christmas song we will begin to learn. These are covers to put your song sheets in, to make your own books. As we learn more songs, we will have more sheets."

She passed out folders of store wrapping paper, each with a scholar's full name written in green ink, in beautiful script, across the top. The girls' books were tied with ribbon to match the ink, the boys' with black shoelaces. Sheets of writing paper were punched with holes to fit the covers. On them, in the same beautiful writing, were the song lyrics.

Chris Chisholm asked shyly, "Miss Jorgensdatter, did you write all them?"

"Yes. Why?"

"They're the purtiest I ever seen. I wisht I could write like that."

Some, like Hartley and Phoebe, who knew better, listened for her to correct Chris's grammar. But she did not. She just smiled at him happily, as though his liking it were important, and said, "Thank you, Chris. I can teach you, if you want to learn. Of course, no one can teach you anything you do not want to learn. But always remember what you write is more important than how you write it. Wise words are the most powerful forces in the world. Can you remember that?"

"Yes'm."

Her hands were busy helping the front-row children fit their papers into their folders.

"Anton Kavell," she smiled, gathering up scattered papers of a new first reader boy. "These are upside down. We better turn them over, because you could not sing very well standing on your head, could you?"

The little ones all laughed together, and Anton watched the teacher with his mouth open, a big grin showing where three teeth were missing.

Meanwhile his big brother, Laddie, looked uneasily at the "Ladislaus Kavel" on his paper. It was a sissy name, he thought, an old-country name. He didn't like people to know his real name. It didn't sound American, he thought. He wanted to stuff the paper into his pocket. He turned it over and looked to see what the Lanceys were doing.

Bart was tying his strings with great care, a smirk on his face. Wade had just stuck the pages inside the cover, without untying the string, and sat frowning into space. Suddenly Alfred Dienstetter, who had no paper, whispered loudly, "If you don't know how, I'll help you," and took the folder from Wade's hand. The boys around looked quickly. Maybe Alfred and Wade were ready to start. But with no signs of smart-alecking, Alfred carefully arranged the punched sheets in their proper place and tied the string. Wade glared but was silent.

Suddenly, the teacher was beside them.

Hepzibah whined, "Teacher, Alfred took Wade's book. Alfred snatched it. I seen him when he done it."

The teacher seemed not to have heard. She smiled at Alfred.

"I am very sorry you did not get one, Alfred. The Dienstetter names were not on the list I had. I have plenty of paper. If you will look on with Wade this time, I will make one for you at recess."

"Aw, that's all right. I was just helpin' Wade here. He didn't know how to get his in without tearin' them."

She smiled again and moved quickly back to the organ. Alfred finished the knot with great care, handed the booklet to Wade, and folded his arms. Wade wore a heavy frown which his brothers knew well, but he never moved. Neither did the Moores. They knew Maureen was watching them, and when Wade was there, he was the leader. If he wasn't starting anything yet, the rest would wait.

They knew these songs already pretty well, and by the

end of the fourth verse of "America" there were some deeper noises coming from the boys' side.

When they had finished "America" Miss Jorgensdatter said, "I think most of you know the next song, 'Star of Wonder, Star of Light' too. We will ask the boys whose voices are deepest to sing the first part, then everyone may join in on star of ... all right? Yes, Gus?"

"If your voice is sometimes deep and sometimes not, when do you sing?"

He got a laugh, which he joined in, but the teacher paid no attention.

"That is a good question, Gus. The answer is to sing with the men if your voice is deep part of the time, because you might as well get used to it. As soon as you are a little older it will be deep all the time."

She was so businesslike about it, the embarrassed fear that had held back even Hartley seemed silly. On signal, the "men" began, at first hesitantly, but soon with growing confidence and strength. After a verse or two they were having a great time. As they finished the last line, Pat Moore called out, "Once again, Teacher."

She smiled, shrugged, and began at the beginning. The older Moores and Lanceys and Laddie had moved into a bunch; they sang out with fervor:

"We three kings of Orient are,
Bearing gifts we traverse afar,
Field and fountain, moor and mountain,
Following yonder star."

But with the beginning of the chorus, the sound was new. High over the voices of the enthusiastic children, rich and clear and ringing, Pat's voice soared:

"Star of mercy, star of light,
Star with royal beauty bright,
Westward leading, still proceeding,
Guide us to the perfect light."

A silence followed, and Pat suddenly became self-conscious and sat down. For once Miss Jorgensdatter looked surprised. Then she began to applaud, and the rest of the school joined in.

When she asked the oldest boys and girls to come forward, there was slouching and grinning, but they all came. She surprised them by handing them books, each with slips of paper.

"I have written out your lesson assignments," she said. "Those of you in the upper grades can go ahead while I start the smaller ones. If you don't understand your lesson, please try to help each other quietly, or find something to do until I get the children started."

With no further attention to them, she moved quickly around the room, gathering up the shy little ones, speaking to each by name, forming a parade line as they held each others' hands. "Make a tail for me," she invited them, and soon they were sitting around the front table, their legs dangling, with slates or paper in front of them. The teacher talked to them softly, writing on their slates, asking them questions even as her eyes seemed to be all over the room.

After a few moments of uncertainty and watching each other, the school settled down to unaccustomed work. Phoebe found herself with a page of hard arithmetic problems. Maureen had some that were easier, but still hard for her. Teacher somehow had seemed to know about where each one was.

Freed of responsibility for the children, and once she had seen that Tessie was busy, Phoebe tackled her job. She soon lost track of the rest of the school. She wrote, washed off her answers, and wrote again. She did not remember very well the long division her father had started to teach her—at first she could not remember which numbers to bring down. But Miss Jorgensdatter said they could help each other. Phoebe got a drink, and then, in passing, put her slate in front of Hartley with the question. He drew arrows from the right numbers to the right places, and soon she found that it began coming back.

Mr. Dawson had given Hartley orders that if there were any signs of trouble, he was to slip out the back and ring the bell. As the day wore on, families on the large circle of homesteads around the schoolhouse listened intently but did not hear the expected call for help. In the middle of the afternoon Mr. Dawson drove slowly past. He watched the school turn out for recess in apparent good order; the teacher joined the younger children in a circle game. As David ran toward the road for a ball, he saw his father, waved happily, and ran back to the circle. A tag game was going, and the big boys seemed to be laying out a fox-and-geese circle. All seemed ideal. But the Dawsons, as well as other parents, waited anxiously for the children to return and report.

This time they did their chores first, gathering cobs, feeding chickens, pigs, cattle and horses, milking and getting in the wood and water as the evening shadows closed in and the wind grew sharper. But as soon as all were gathered around the table and they had said the blessing, their father asked,

"Well, what do you think? Can she keep school?"

Phoebe looked at Hartley. "What do you think? You were with the Lanceys, the Moores, and Laddie Kavel and the Dienstetters."

Hartley thoughtfully drowned a large potato with gravy and took a big bite while he seriously considered. Finally he answered, "I don't know."

Impatiently their father asked, "Well, how do they seem? Are they looking for trouble? Or settling down?"

"Wel-l-l I sort of think the Moores just want a little fun, you know how they like to tease and joke. But she doesn't get mad, so it's not much fun to tease her. Pat once was whispering real loud, telling a joke; instead of saying she would lick him or anything, she stopped the whole school, and asked him, real polite, to come to the front. Then she said to the whole school, 'Mr. Moore has something important to say, so important it can't wait until recess. So please pay courteous attention. Mr. Moore, you may feel free to speak as long as you need to.' And she took out her watch that she wears around her neck and said 'Now, begin.'"

All the children laughed at the memory.

"Old Pat was surprised, you can believe. He stood there, and everyone was looking at him, and he stood on one foot and then the other, like an old goose. Tad Kavel giggled, and the teacher very quietly said, 'Hush, Tad. It is Mr. Moore's turn to speak.' And we waited and waited. Finally Irene asked right out loud, 'Why don't you say something, Pat?' Old Pat got red, and sort of barked, 'Got nothing to say.' Miss Jorgensdatter said, very polite like, 'Thank you, Pat. And the next time you need to make a speech, please raise your hand for permission first.'"

Hartley laughed again. "Old Pat said at noon he never wanted to go through that again, and he had learned one thing for sure—he was never going to run for office."

"You think you all learned something about not whispering and disturbing the school?"

"Well, most of us, I guess. And about a lot of things. And it was fun, especially singing. But I think ..."

"Yes?"

"I think Wade is sort of boiling inside."

Phoebe nodded. "That was what I thought. When he seemed about to blow up, she would be right there, asking him politely to do something, and he always did. But I think he was madder every time."

"What about Bart?"

Tessie giggled, and Phoebe joined in. "Bart just about spent all day combing his hair, and at first recess he cleaned

112

his fingernails. I think Bart wants her to like him. But Laddie Kavel—he and Wade look at each other, and ..."

Hartley added, "They keep daring each other. Anton Kavel said Laddie and Wade was playing cards with some of the fellows that go to Texas, and they have a bet on that no girl schoolteacher is going to boss them."

Mrs. Dawson sighed. "I feared as much. What can be done?"

"I don't know of anything yet, Marian. She insisted on doing it her own way, and at least she seems to have come out on top the first day. But I want you all to understand: There is probably trouble coming, and when it does, I want none of you mixed up in it. Is that clear? Hartley?"

"I'm not going to make any trouble! She's going to have a Christmas program, and we will sing and all say poems and pieces, and we are going to organize a government and elect officers!" Hartley said excitedly.

"The girls, too," Tessie added. "All the girls will vote, just like anyone else. To get in practice for when women get the vote."

"I know one thing," Hartley went on. "I think she knows somehow that Wade can't read. Because when she gave out the lessons, she gave him a handmade book of pieces of paper tied together. It had catalog pictures of horses, cows, a plow share, a windmill and an axle and stuff like that pasted on it. The name of each one was written and printed beside it. She said for him to write the names on his slate, and be able to spell them and say them without the pictures. And she did it just private, to him."

Mr. and Mrs. Dawson looked at each other. Then Mrs. Dawson asked, "What did Wade do?"

"That's how come I knew about it. He asked if he could sit with me, and she let him. He showed me and wanted to see if he had them right before she called him to recite. She took him by himself—Maureen, too—I mean, by herself.

Anyway, Wade worked on them hard. He knew them pretty well. But he looked awful mad all the time he was doing it."

The younger children thought school was wonderful.

David said, "Hepzibah and Irene and Ellen and Anton and Abe and me did colors, with pieces of cloth. We did blue and green and red and—what was that funny one?"

"Plaid," Robbie helped him.

"I remember—p-l-a-i-d. That's all kinds of colors cross-ways."

"And Tessie, did you learn something, too?" their mother asked, relieved that Tessie seemed to have forgotten her mourning for Mr. Gould.

"Oh yes, we had mostly history. I learned that lots of women were important right here in this country already. One named Anne Hutchins helped get religious freedom. And Mrs. Anne Bradstreet had eight children and was the first good American poet and both of them lived Back East, before George Washington. Another woman, Mrs. Mary Ann Bickerdyke, right here in Kansas, is still alive. She had a bunch of children and was a sort of doctor that told General Grant how to take care of sick soldiers. She was called a general and went everywhere with the soldiers in our war, and then she was the attorney to get pay called 'pensions' for the soldiers after they came home. She planned how the government should give them extra help to get homesteads too. There are lots more important women and some of them are not named Anne. They have children and are good mothers and they do important things just the same. I am going to be an important woman too. Please pass the apple butter."

Both parents jumped at that announcement from their shy daughter. They looked at Phoebe, who shrugged and smiled and passed the apple butter.

By the end of the first week, the school seemed to be settling into a steady routine. There was the usual whispering, which was all right with the teacher if it was not interrupting someone else rudely when everyone was supposed to be paying attention. There were mild fights, mostly between brothers and sisters. Once some of the middle group took too long on a fox hunt at noon and came in late. But the teacher stayed calm and firm and let them make up the time at recess. She seemed to show up in time to separate people and start them on something different before things got serious. Everyone seemed satisfied enough except Laddie Kavell and Wade Lancey.

There was nothing exactly to report, Hartley and Phoebe agreed, and they did not want to be tattletales. But Wade and Laddie stood up last, sat down last, dropped things and coughed a lot. People going past them seemed to trip a lot. Most of all, they said things in undertones to each other and grinned. But although the teacher seemed to see everything else going on in the room, even when her back was turned, she never seemed to notice anything wrong with them.

Maureen confided to Phoebe, "Sure, I think she's a grand lady, and kind, the way she is teaching me to read and cipher. She never giving me shame because she's so much smarter than I am. But still, I don't think she's fair, the way she keeps strict order with everyone else and never has eyes in her head for what those two are up to."

"Well, I think she is just waiting. If it was me, I'd know I couldn't do anything to them, and I'd wait until they got worse and did something real bad, and then I could put them out." Phoebe said.

At the beginning of the second week the two big boys seemed to have a special secret. They stayed away from the others at recesses and even their little brothers didn't know what was up. Everyone felt something was going to happen. It did, but not what they expected.

At noon the teacher had the little children eat with her at the recitation table where they took turns reading to each other. Then they went out to play when the others came in.

The older and middle girls decided to take a walk along the firebreak toward the creek. The warm spell had melted most of the snow, but some lingered in the muddy, shady strips along the hedge. The girls were looking for animal tracks—rabbits, squirrels, coyotes—keeping the nature diary they had started with Mr. Gould. They talked of clothes styles and egg money and their plans for the Christmas program. The time passed. Suddenly they realized it was probably getting late. They let the smaller ones start first, and then raced for the school.

When they arrived, they found all the boys laughing, breathless and excited. The side of the school was covered with the green and brown stains of muddy hedge apples.

The fat, green, half-rotten hedge apples were scattered under the trees. Later, no one was sure how the game had started. Wade and Laddie were in the middle seeing who could come closest to hitting a spot someone had made. They had their caps full of hedge apples. The other boys ran to get their own ammunition and start their own spots. When the girls arrived, the whole side of the building was a mess.

Phoebe exclaimed, horrified, "Hartley!"

Maureen cried out, "Sean! and you, Pat. And Mike?"

The rest of the girls joined in, and the boys began hushing them.

"Just look what you have done to the school!"

Gus tried to brush off a spot with the sleeve of his jacket. It just smeared.

Wade laughed. "What do you mean, 'what we've done.' Did you see anyone do anything?"

"N-no," they admitted. They had not actually seen anyone throw anything.

"All right, then. Suppose you stupid girls mind your own business for once."

All of them moved quietly to the front of the building. The teacher, smiling her usual greeting, shooed out the little ones for their play. The others filed in even before she had signaled for Sean to ring the bell.

With unusual speed everyone in the building hung up wraps and began to work hard on something. The teacher had just called the top arithmetic class, which included Phoebe and Hartley, when the little children came running in, calling, "Teacher! Teacher! Come see what happened to the schoolhouse!"

Miss Jorgensdatter looked sharply at all those in front of her. Some were looking at the excited children, some at her. In the back seats a half-dozen very studious young men never raised their eyes from their books and slates. She went out fast—the chattering children leading the way—and she came back fast. Her eyes flashed and her voice snapped.

"Attention please everyone!"

Wade and Laddie seemed too busy to hear. She did not speak their names, but just looked at them and waited. Everyone else looked too. Finally, in the silence, the boys got nervous and looked up.

"I want you to tell me what you know about the stains on the side of the schoolhouse. I will begin with the oldest. Wade Lancey?"

"Stains? What stains?" Wade grinned and lolled back in his seat.

"You know nothing of any stains on the schoolhouse?"

"I said, 'what stains?'"

"Ladislaus Kavell?"

"I don't know what you mean. I'm just sittin' here doin' my jogerphy."

One by one, she asked each boy in the room. Some of the younger ones seemed about to speak up, then they looked at Laddie and Wade, who were glowering at them, and each one echoed, "Not me."

When Hartley paused, and then said, like the others "Not me," Phoebe gasped.

Hartley met her glare as the teacher went on to Gus, Gopher, Sean, and finally the Dienstetter twins. When she had finished, Hartley bit his lips and raised his hand.

"Miss Jorgensdatter, I guess I did it," he said very low.

She looked at him intently. "Alone?"

He diverted his eyes from hers as he answered, "Yes."

At that there were assorted murmurings from the girls' side. Then Gus, Gopher, and finally Sean raised their hands and said they had helped.

Very courteously, then, the teacher said, "Perhaps the rest of you have improved memories now. Did any other boy throw anything at the schoolhouse?"

All was silent. Phoebe and Maureen could hardly hold in their indignation, but both knew their brothers would not want them to interfere. Maureen sputtered, in a whisper, "It's not fair!" and this time Phoebe agreed.

Miss Jorgensdatter seemed to grow taller in front of their eyes. She turned to the girls' side and said sternly, "It is quite clear that these four boys could not have accomplished such a thorough job alone. I think they have confessed gallantly in order to protect the real culprits—the people who really did the damage."

A breath-sucking sound suddenly erupted from the back of the boys' side. The teacher paid no attention.

She looked straight at Phoebe. "If these boys are taking the blame for someone weaker and more helpless than they," which prompted another noise, almost a groan, from the older boys' corner, "it must be you older girls they are protecting, because the little children were in here with me."

This time there was a sort of squeak from the boys.

Maureen tensed, ready to spring.

Phoebe held her, whispering, "Look at her! I think she's up to something."

The teacher continued, "I do not understand why you would want to spoil your beautiful new white schoolhouse.

But I know that young ladies like you are already sorry, so I will not ask you. A real lady keeps herself and her home as clean and attractive as she possibly can, and for most of the week this is our house.

"Only pigs live in pigpens. So, the mess must be cleaned up. The boys who have admitted to throwing dirt will help, too, so that the gentlemen who did not have anything to do with such babyish bad manners will have the privilege of pursuing their education indoors, while we girls clean the paint."

Phoebe squeezed Maureen's hand, and Maureen squeezed back. Tessie flashed a grin back at them, and Helga Dienstetter was almost laughing. Teacher had said, "we girls." Whatever she planned, they were eager to go along with it.

Phoebe turned to see how the culprits were taking being called "babies." When she caught Wade's sheepish look, she laughed out loud. The teacher continued calmly.

"Tomorrow, each girl bring a bucket, soap and rags or brushes or brooms—whatever you can that will be useful. I will borrow ladders. We will spend the day making our school again a place we can be proud of, instead of one the other districts can call an infant school and laugh at."

That remark got to the boys. They had not exactly thought of what Texas School might say about the brownish-green stains.

All the girls were sure now that she knew that they had had no part in the trouble. Hartley began breathing more freely as he realized that he was not going to be made the scapegoat. Some of the other boys began to realize that scrubbing paint—the whole crowd of them outside in the warm December sunshine that promised to hold for at least another day—was a much pleasanter prospect than studying inside.

Pat raised his hand. "Miss Jorgensdatter, I threw some of the stuff too."

"I did too," Mike joined in.

Several others added, "Me too." But not Laddie or Wade.

"Boys," she said serenely, "I appreciate your chivalry in trying to help the girls take their punishment. But I do not want you to perjure yourselves, even for a good cause. Girls are citizens too. Every citizen must stand the consequences of his or her own deeds. I am sure none of the girls would want you to miss part of your studies to make up for what they did.

"You will each have individual assignments for all day tomorrow. I feel it is my duty to be with the girls, who seem to need closer supervision than I have given them so far. So I will not be able to hear any recitations—you will write them out."

A blow, indeed! A whole day of writing!

The girls began to look forward to the break in the routine. They enjoyed the way Miss Jorgensdatter was putting something over on those smarty boys. Nevertheless, they felt resentful at having to clean what the boys had done. Every boy with a sister had to face an angry report at home.

The next morning Miss Jorgensdatter, wearing an old brown calico dress and apron and a man's shabby jacket arrived driving a wagon borrowed from Mr. Hackett. In it were two ladders, some extra buckets, some soap and brushes. She brought a pair of corn-shucking gloves to protect her hands and a knit cap to cover her braids.

The girls agreed, "Clothes aren't so important, really. Even in that outfit, she looks like a queen."

Opening exercises were short. Then each of the big boys received a paper with his name on it and his day's assignment in each of his studies. Surprisingly, both Wade and Laddie were present. Anton said Laddie was going to play hooky; Wade's father was making him come. Wade had called Laddie yellow; they had a fight. The rumor was that

Laddie lost and Wade made him come. However it happened both were there, and both were silent.

"These assignments will take a month!" Pat complained. Kurt Dienstetter, usually quiet, laughed. "Not for me. I'm going to finish fast so I have time to go help the teacher." Wade then growled, but Mike said, "Wait. What's yours say at the end?"

They all looked, then—and read the same as Mike had.

"When you have finished your assignments, turn to page 379 in the history book and copy the Constitution of the United States until the dismissal bell."

Alfred Dienstetter groaned out loud. Miss Jorgensdatter, hustling about with the girls, heard and turned.

"Are you ill, Alfred?" she asked anxiously. "Should I send Hartley on his horse to get your father to drive you to the doctor?"

By now Alfred knew she was just the woman to do it, and he knew well enough the trouble he would be in at home. No one ever went to the doctor except in emergencies. Even then the expense was an awful worry. He protested quickly, "Oh, no, ma'am. I feel fine!"

"I hope you are not being foolishly brave. It does not pay to take chances with a pain so bad that it makes a strong man groan out loud." She waited expectantly, her head tilted, her pen raised over paper to write a note to his father. Someone giggled at the phrase, "strong man" but the teacher did not hear. Her sharp eyes were fixed on Alfred.

"No ma'am, I feel fine!"

"Very well."

Quietly the other boys began getting out their slates and tablets. Laddie Kavell made one final try. "I haven't that much room on my slate, and I haven't much paper in my tablet."

But the teacher was ready. "Here is paper you may use. It is used paper from the *Walnut Valley Times*—the editor has been saving it for me. It is only used on one side. You use the other."

She brought a stack of paper from her drawer and laid it on top of the desk.

That was the last straw: they gave in. Meanwhile the girls and the four boys, with the little children, who were told they could play or help as they wished, began sloshing happily outside the windows.

When Bart strolled to the window to see what was going on, Miss Jorgensdatter appeared inside at once. She said, "I am very sorry I underestimated your speed, Bart. I did not intend to make you waste school time just loafing. Here is some additional work to keep you busy." She began writing rapidly on his assignment paper.

He protested, "But I'm not done with what you gave me."

Her eyes widened. "Oh, I thought you must be—or you wouldn't have been wasting time."

At noon Miss Jorgensdatter told the boys they could eat in their seats, and not waste valuable time on noon recess. Those who were being punished got to eat on the steps of the shed, where the buildings protected them from the wind. The sun pouring down on them made for a pleasant December picnic.

The scrubbers sang all morning. First, "This is the way we scrub our school, scrub our school, scrub our school," then party songs, and church songs. The boys inside heard the teacher telling a story; they could not hear well enough to follow it, but they could hear the workers laughing gaily every few minutes. It became harder and harder to keep their minds on long division and history dates.

At noon, when those inside discovered that Miss Jorgensdatter had brought out a huge freezer of ice cream and two big cakes from the wagon and was serving the treats to the workers, they were furious. While she explained to the workers that with their extra physical labor they needed extra nourishment, the boys inside boiled with jealousy.

"You, Wade Lancey, with your smart ideas," Mike growled. "Catch me being such a fool again."

"You're a fool all the time—Shanty Irish!" Bart retorted. Strangely, Wade said nothing. But Pat and Mike both started to jump Bart. Laddie stepped in.

"Hold it! And shut up, Bart, with your names. People from other places are as good or better as anyone who just happened to be born American. Anyway, she's the one we want to get even with. Save your fight for her."

Wade looked up. "You'll never get even with her." His manner was strange. "She always thinks like a buzz saw, while you're feeling your way with both hands."

Puzzled, the boys looked at him, then got drinks and settled back to work. They had all had all the trouble at home they wanted for quite a while, and they knew there had better not be notes go home that they had not done their lessons as told.

The shadows grew longer; the dark reflection of the building on the ground was almost due east as the workers stood back to inspect.

"Even with lye soap and hard rubbing, you can see where the stains were," they agreed.

"At least," the teacher said, "we have soaped and scrubbed and rinsed all the surface. When it is spring, we will try to get hold of some paint, and paint it over. For now we have done the best we can. You might as well take a recess until dismissal. I will see if the boys need any help."

As Hartley rang the last bell and went to bridle the horses, the older boys sullenly filed out, called crossly to brothers and sisters and pulled out of the schoolyard promptly. Until the turn-off, the Dawsons could hear Pat and Mike, in the wagon behind them, telling the rest of the family to hold their whist at home, while the rest of the Moores chattered gaily on about what fun they had had and how good the ice cream and cake were.

The next morning the teacher started school as usual, acting as though the day before had never been. She pointed to a new stack of newspapers and magazines on her desk.

"These are copies of the *Wichita Eagle*, the *Kansas City Star* and the *Walnut Valley Times*, Kansas papers some of your families take. And these are some copies of *Frank Leslie's Illustrated Newspaper*, with lots of pictures, and *Harper's Magazine*. The magazines are harder reading, without pictures, but they have some interesting ideas.

"There are also three magazines from Back East made especially for children: *The Youth's Companion*, *Merry's Museum*, edited by Louisa May Alcott—some of you enjoyed the books she wrote, *Little Women* and *Little Men*—and this is *St. Nicholas Magazine*, edited by a woman named Mary Mapes Dodge. She wrote *Hans Brinker*, or *The Silver Skates*, a very interesting story about two Dutch children who skated on ice on canals they have in Holland instead of streets. Maybe soon we can get a copy. Meanwhile, I want each of you to look through these, find something you like, read it, and be ready to tell the rest of the class about it Friday afternoon. We will practice public speaking then to get ready for our Christmas program, when all the patrons come. This Friday we will be our own audience, and listen to each other."

Kurt Dienstetter murmured, in what he thought was a low tone, "I'd druther clean the pig pen than listen to all that gab."

But she heard. Pleasantly she said, "Very well, Kurt. I will write your father that you will be dismissed at noon Friday to clean the pig pen."

There were no more protests. Kurt said he had changed his mind, but she silently gave him the note.

The next morning his brother kept urging him, "You better give the teacher the note."

Finally he raised his hand, took a torn piece of tablet paper to the teacher, and kicked his brother under the seat.

"What's it say?" Sean whispered.

Alfred grinned and answered in spite of Kurt's threatening gestures. "It says, 'No Dienstetter talks smarty to teacher. Kurt can clean pig pen before Friday afternoon. When is school, Kurt is in school. With mouth shut.'"

After their experiences of standing before the entire school and speaking, or singing, they began to get excited about the Christmas program, when everyone in the community would come. They decided that first they would decorate a Christmas tree.

"First we got to get a tree," they agreed. Wade was absent all week. He was supposed to cut a small cottonwood for them. Bart volunteered. He had plenty of help, and the boys brought in a nicely shaped tree, strong in the trunk and with some fair sized branches. Without directions from the teacher, they cut it to fit between the ceiling and floor and made a cross-bar frame to hold it upright.

Once the tree was standing steady in the front corner of the school, with the recitation table moved to the back to make room, Christmas seemed to have started, although there were still three weeks to wait. Every morning there were new ideas, new materials brought from home, new reasons for rushing through lessons.

Several families, including the Osbornes, who had no children, donated packages of carded, washed and bleached wool. Taller children, with flour-and-water paste, climbed ladders to begin at the top branches, carefully fastening small bits of wool to the bark to look like snow. When the snowstorm was complete, they began decorating with everything bright they could think of. Some brought saved hoards of tinfoil, bright paper bits from wrappings from Back East, or home-dyed pieces of cloth. They covered black walnuts with paper or cloth and hung them on black threads from branches. Some brought cattails dipped in red barn paint and dried grasses dipped in melted wax.

"Keep them away from the stove—they will melt easily," Miss Jorgensdatter gently admonished.

Hartley had several dozen new, large nails which, on their invisible black threads, looked like fireflies on a summer night flying free around the tree. Gus polished up all the old brass harness rings he could find and tied them up too.

"We got silver and gold just like the Orient kings!"

The little children cut newspapers into strips, pasting the strips together with flour-and-water paste to form endless chains. With mulberry juice they colored some red; bluing water made some blue. "What can we use to make green?" Laddie wondered.

"Hedge apples!" Maureen taunted. Laddie threw the nearest thing, which was a small pan of paste. It was not a heavy pan, but the paste was sticky, of course, and it landed on her hair. But Maureen laughed. Laddie laughed too, then offered to go with her to pump water for her to wash it off. They were gone quite awhile, but the teacher did not seem to mind.

In the end there were no hedge-apple green decorations.

One morning the Pfitzers, with great excitement, carried in a good-sized box and placed it carefully on the teacher's desk.

"Stand back! Don't break it! Careful, Gus," his siblings urged. Gus proudly pulled out piles of shredded paper packing and then lost courage.

"You do it, teacher."

She looked, gasped, and with due reverence took out a breathtakingly beautiful angel of spun glass.

"Meine mutter—I mean my mother—brought it from her home in Bavaria," Gus said proudly.

"I thought you were from Germany," Chris said.

"Bavaria is Germany, stupid! Look at the map! She says at her home there are lots of trees that stay green all winter. They have little needles instead of leaves and they are the real Christmas trees."

"Ours is real! How could we paste snow on if it wasn't?" Chris argued.

"Anyway, her brothers and uncles and lots of the family make pretty little animals and angels and things like this. They melt the glass and blow it with a pipe, and they know how to make it go in different shapes. But they break awful easy traveling, so this was all she could bring."

Miss Jorgensdatter stood guard before the excited children. "This is indeed a treasure. In my home, too, we had some spun glass ornaments for the Christmas tree. It is very generous of Mrs. Pfitzer to let us use this. Come look at it, one at a time. Look with your eyes, not with your hands. When everyone has had a turn we will ask Mike to put it high on top of the organ, where it will be safe until Christmas."

While Mike was lifting the repacked box someone remembered that Wade was even taller than Mike and asked, "Where's Wade?"

Bart shrugged. "Home, I guess. Said he was too old for school. Pa said not till he's twenty-one, that's not till summer, and he had to come. But Wade said. 'No.' Then Pa licked him with a harness strap, but Wade said lickin' won't make him come back."

"Well, I'm glad," Sean said. "Aren't you, Teacher?"

"No," she said firmly. "No. I am very sorry. Please tell Wade, Bart, that I said I wished he would come back. No one is ever too old to go to school."

"He says he started too late."

"Tell him I said a late start is no excuse for quitting. It is just a reason to go faster."

The next Monday Wade showed up again, driving the wagon into the schoolyard in plenty of time for his brothers to reach their seats. But as Gopher, after ringing the last bell, came in, Wade's seat still was empty.

"He's not coming in," the whisper went around.

Then, as the teacher started to read the Bible verses, the door slammed again and Wade lounged in noisily. He did not go around to the outside aisle, but down the middle, making all the boys in his row stand to let him in. He dropped his slate, slowly picked it up, dropped two books, picked them up, then replaced them inside the desk and let the top drop noisily. Miss Jorgensdatter waited, her eyes never leaving him. But he did not look up.

When he finally seemed settled, he looked around, then grinned.

"Mr. Lancey, you are late!" the teacher said sternly.

"Trouble with the horses," Wade's laugh was taunting. "Old plugs got horse sense. I guess they don't like school."

She looked at him a long minute. He looked right back. The room was silent. She began to read.

Laddie wrote on his slate and slipped it down the row to Hartley and the Moores. "The Texas fellers laffed at Wade for lettin' a girl teacher run him out, and he bet them he wood run her out this weak. But he's gone yeller. I knowd he wood."

Pat wrote underneath, "the week ain't over" and passed it back.

In the quiet of the first period after recess, Wade, without asking permission, stood up, clumped noisily to the water bucket, took a long drink with loud slurps, dropped the dipper, picked it up from the floor and dropped it back into the bucket without even wiping it off. He then started back to his seat as though nothing was unusual.

Miss Jorgensdatter was with the upper-grade class diagramming sentences on the blackboard. She came to attention at the first disturbance, but she watched silently, until he shoved the other boys and sat down. Everyone waited. She waited, again a long minute. Then she said in a strange voice, "Wade Lancey, will you please come to the front of the room?"

"Why, sure," he laughed again, and slowly lounged toward the front.

Usually when she called someone up for punishment, Miss Jorgensdatter spoke quietly, so that only the wrong-doer could hear. But now she let her voice carry to all the listening ears. "I need not list all the things you have done to be rude and disturb this school. You know them as well as I do. But I will give you a chance to apologize."

Wade shoved his hands down in his pockets, stepped nearer to her, looked down slightly to meet her eyes, and laughed. "You said I should come back. You want me to apologize for that? I was thirsty. You want me to apologize for that? Now, with that whole bucketful of water and a 150-foot well full besides, that don't hardly seem sensible, does it?"

"Are you going to apologize?"

A long, drawn-out, breathless silence followed; neither pair of eyes flinched. Then he grinned at her, and said not loud, but very clear, "Nope." Without permission he swung around, and sauntered toward his seat.

Nothing happened. The teacher turned quickly back to the board and began drawing lines around words in the sentence she had written. As Wade passed the tense little boys on the front row, he rather playfully reached out and pushed Abe's head just as Anton, next to him, moved. The heads bumped, and both boys cried out. The teacher turned again. Wade was back in his seat. She looked at the two little boys who had made the noise.

"We cannot have this continued disturbance. Wade Lancey, you step outside and cut a hedge switch for me."

Maureen's eyes blazed. "Well, what do you say about being fair now?"

Phoebe's eyes were filled with tears.

"I didn't think she would be like that—backing down from Wade and then whipping the little boys."

"Maybe she won't whip them hard."

But when Wade came in with a wispy switch, she said firmly, "That is not satisfactory. I want one at least as big as your finger."

At that there was a murmur through the room. Anton began to whimper, and Abe put his head in his hands. Wade frowned, but after a pause, he went back out. He brought a sturdy switch as she had said.

"That good enough?" he said roughly.

She tried it on the air a couple of times, testing it to make sure it had not been cut in the middle, and then said calmly, "This will be fine."

Wade moved over to his brother, took a grip on his shoulder and then moved back, watching.

"Oh, Wade—stay here."

His surprise showed.

"I want you to do the whipping." Her voice was hard. For once, she did not say "please."

Wade was clearly upset. He looked at the whimpering boys, glanced around at the other scholars and turned quickly away from their angry faces. Laddie Kavel looked ready to spring at the first lick at Anton. Wade turned back to the teacher and met her eyes, which were hard and determined. He was puzzled. She said she wanted him to do the whipping but she was unbuttoning her cuff, carefully rolling up her sleeve above the elbow. "Maybe," he thought in relief that showed in his face, "she has changed her mind and is going to do the whipping herself."

Wade's thoughts were interrupted by Miss Jorgensdatter's calm voice. "Wade Lancey, it is my responsibility to your parents, to your country, and to you to teach you not only to read and cipher but, as long as you are a scholar and I am a teacher, I am supposed to teach you to have respect for other people, especially those younger and weaker than you. Bullying is a cowardly trait. The West has no place for cowards.

"It is clear that I am failing in my duty, and therefore I should be punished. Your actions show that you, more than the others, have suffered from my failure to teach you how a man should behave. Therefore it is your place to punish me."

She took the switch from under her arm and handed it back to him with such a glare that he let his hand close on it. He was breathing hard, his eyes wide, ("like a scared horse" the children said later). He stood frozen as she held out her white, bare arm closer and closer to him.

"Three strikes. Hit it! With your full arm, Wade. You are a grown, strong man. You can do a good job. Hit!"

Everyone cowered. Never had they heard anything that went through them like her words. And still Wade stood, holding the switch, looking at the white wrist, forearm, elbow and above as though he were dazed.

Slowly he looked up. Standing up straight, Wade looked down with his dark eyes and met hers. It was a long, tense moment—her blazing blue-green eyes never swerved. Phoebe felt a scream rising in her throat and pushed it back with her hands. Just then Wade's mouth trembled, and he looked aside.

In a broken, deep voice, he exclaimed, "Dang!" and turned away. He raised one knee, broke the hedge stick over it with a relieving crack—and then another, and another. As he broke that stick into the smallest pieces his hands could get hold of he took long, hard strides toward the stove, where he banged open the door, threw in the pieces, and slammed the door shut again.

There were sounds of breathing again, but little else. The teacher had not moved, except that her arm had dropped to her side, and she was limp.

Suddenly the heavy silence was shattered by Wade's stern voice. "All right, get to work, all of you. You're here to learn, not to have a circus. Get busy!" Very deliberately he walked down the outside aisle, slid into his seat, picked out of his desk the paper book of pictures and words and with lips set, looked at nothing else.

He curled his big hand carefully around the slim slate pencil and silently began to copy the letters.

CHAPTER SEVEN

A FREEDOM DISTRICT CHRISTMAS

*T*ONIGHT WAS THE night! They had thought it would never come—the first Christmas program at Freedom School. The warm spell had held, the night air was soft, and the sky was a ceiling of stars. The yellowed flame of the lantern swinging at the front of the wagon tongue cast shifting shadows on the high, bent prairie grass, but all the young Dawsons, cuddled together under robes and quilts on straw bedding in the wagon bed, saw only the clear stars twinkling at them from edge to edge of the heavens.

The bell had been steadily ringing for half an hour.

"It's calling, 'come, come, come,'" David said.

"Look!" Robbie pointed to another glimmering light at ground level.

"It must be the Moores," their father decided. As they came closer to the schoolhouse, other lights began appearing in ones and twos, coming from all directions across the prairie toward the welcoming, lighted windows of the building.

"I'll bet God thinks it looks like a star on earth, with all the rays pointing out ever which way," Tessie added.

"That's an interesting idea, Tessie," their father said.

"People have always talked of knowledge as being like a light that shines on those around and shows them the way. Here, the school is for knowledge, but the little lights are coming to it to make it bigger."

Voices grew louder as the groups came closer. The school seemed strange at night, with so many people crowding into the schoolyard and unloading wagons all around the building. Children greeted each other as if they had been apart for weeks instead of a few hours. Mothers unwrapped babies; shy, curious toddlers peeked from their mothers' skirts. The schoolchildren, who belonged, were so consumed with excitement they were ready to explode.

"See!" Tessie pointed out to her parents, "look above the teacher's desk."

They saw a long board, painted black, with huge white words standing out, "Ad Astra Per Aspera."

"That's the state motto, and it's Latin. Chris, Sean, Jim and I did it all by ourselves. It means 'to the stars through difficulty,' because Kansas had so much trouble getting to be a state and earning a star on the flag," Tessie said proudly.

"What are the words made of?" her mother wanted to know. "They seem to stand out."

"Popcorn! Gus painted the board, then we drew the letters with a ruler and pencil and filled them in with paste and popcorn."

The Christmas tree drew gasps of admiration and started a few tears of homesickness among the parents, who thought of faraway places where there were green trees and holly. This one filled its corner with a soft glow of light from the dozens of beeswax candles made by the children, all of which were fitted into old-country candleholders that the teacher had brought. The tiny wisps of white wool did look almost like snow, although Mr. Pfitzer was heard to remark that in his country snow seldom stuck like that on the underside of branches. Hartley's nails and Gus's harness rings swung merrily, and above it all the wonderful Christmas angel smiled down on everyone.

Fancy-shaped cookies—gingerbread boys and girls, stars, angels, and animals—floated in the air around the tree, their black threads invisible in the dim light. Underneath the tree on a draped white sheet glowed an orange pile—real oranges! They appeared after the children went home in the afternoon and now caused excited, curious questions. But the teacher just smiled.

As wagon after wagon of people unloaded, piles of other mysterious packages and sacks began to appear around the base of the tree until the suspense was almost too much to bear.

The big boys, taking turns, had kept the bell ringing constantly. People talked over it; here and there a child whimpered. Scholars busy behind the sheets hung on wires across the front directed each other to "move this" or "stand back there" until the noise mounted higher and higher. The stove door clanged at intervals as men added more sticks of wood until the sides of the stove glowed red. New arrivals clustered around it, stamping feet and rubbing hands to get warmed.

Tessie, in the aisle beside her mother, said, "Just think, in all the thousands of years this earth has been born, there has never before been this much noise right here."

Suddenly the bell stopped. At once the children stopped except for a hissing that spread like a dud firecracker. A hush of expectation fell on the audience as people packed as closely as possible to make room for latecomers. Those who were standing made themselves comfortable against the walls.

When all was quiet, the sheets in front parted and the teacher stepped out. An admiring murmur filled the room.

A child's voice was heard above the hush.

"Mum, is that the Christmas angel?"

"Yes, dear. Be quiet."

She was wearing her blue-green dress. The light from the lantern swinging overhead reflected on her yellow-red hair in its braided crown, and in back someone whistled.

The teacher smiled and said simply, in her clear, carrying voice, "Friends, we welcome you to the first Christmas program of Freedom School District. Your children have worked hard to give you a jolly evening. I wish each of you a merry, merry Christmas. Now I will turn the program over to our master of ceremonies, the newly elected mayor of our school, Mr. Wade Lancey."

A louder murmur arose which stilled when Wade appeared. His nervousness showed only in the tightly clenched fists held firmly at his sides. He wore the store suit his father had been married in. It was tight for Wade, but he stood tall. In a gesture of habit he shook back his hair—unnecessary now because his usually untidy locks were firmly plastered to his head.

Clearing his throat he said clearly, if a little stiffly, "Welcome to the Freedom District Christmas program. The first number will feature Tessie Dawson as Mary; Sean Moore as Joseph; Robbie Dawson, Gus Pfitzer, and Gopher, I mean Edward Martin, as shepherds; Kurt Dienstetter, Brad Lancey and Mike Moore as wise men, and, and ..."

After a whisper from behind him he concluded, "and Pat Moore as the innkeeper and Hartley Dawson as King Herod. This is called, 'A Night in Bethlehem.'"

As he stepped back, the organ softly began the strains of "Silent Night." David Dawson and Ellen Moore appeared, and, signaling each other, carefully pulled back a sheet suspended on wire to reveal an innkeeper behind a wooden counter carefully polishing a glass. A crooked sign identified the setting as the Bethlehem Inn.

Two travelers entered: the woman wrapped in a blue shawl, the man with a towel tied around his head.

The travelers were turned away decisively.

The curtain pullers closed the curtains briefly then opened them again after a loud voice whispered, "Now!"

This time the travelers appeared seated on piles of straw. Behind them was a manger with some straggly cornhusks caught in the sides and a white wrapped bundle in it.

Shepherds arrived in sheepskin jackets, carrying authentic crooks and a lamb. They announced that they had seen angels and a big star and were sent to see the new baby.

Wise men arrived wearing bathrobes. Around their heads were scarves trimmed with cutout tin pieces. One of them forgot exactly what he had seen, but with a little help from his friends finally remembered; all of them presented gifts and were leaving when loud noises erupted in the rear.

King Herod, wearing a high, woven straw crown that threatened to fall off unless he held it with one hand, stopped the departing wise men and demanded to be taken to the new king. Joseph and the shepherds quickly closed ranks. Mary crouched over the manger, the wise men began shouting and the lamb bleated, all at the same time:

"He's gone!"

"They went thataway."

"He ain't here."

"Ba-a-a-"

At that moment the audience and actors alike were startled by an unexpected sound: the sharp "W-a-a-a!" from the bundle in the manger. Apparently frightened by the loud noises, the unidentified actor yelled louder and thrust his tiny fists in the air. Herod as well as the worshippers stood paralyzed until a woman's voice from the audience called, "Pick him up, Tessie. He won't shut up till you do."

Mary obediently picked up the baby, who instantly stopped yelling. Laughing, he firmly grasped Tessie's hair and gazed out upon the curious people surrounding him.

A loud whisper from behind called, "David, Ellen, close the curtains." The audience broke into laughing applause and foot-stamping, which brought on renewed howls from behind the curtains until Mary brought the protesting infant down to his laughing mother.

After a short interval the mayor reappeared to announce a group of songs by the entire school. Some duets followed, then Pat Moore sang a solo that brought loud applause and some encouraging remarks from the audience.

Again after some slight consultation backstage, the

mayor, relaxed and at ease now, announced, "I reckon that's all for tonight, folks."

A roar of protest, led by the scholars onstage and echoed by the little children out front, drowned him out. The mayor looked surprised. As he protested to the children the general bustle was interrupted by the vigorous shaking of sleigh bells at the rear. A loud, deep voice laughed from the door, eliciting frenzied shouts of those nearby.

"It's Santa Claus! Merry Christmas!"

Santa it was, with a long white beard and a snowy head of hair covered with a red stocking cap. Strips of white wool batting stuck out of his cuffs and the front of his red wool jacket, which did not quite meet in front, revealing a bit of brown work shirt. His wide, black leather belt held the jacket in place as he stomped up the aisle in his worn, high-heeled riding boots shouting "Ho! Ho! Ho!"

Tiny children hid in fear, older ones affirmed their bravery by staring, and the adults began laughing and shouting back, "Merry Christmas, Santa."

Some man's voice was heard to comment, "Looks more like a fat sheep to me, all that wool!" Santa looked at him and laughed again. On his shoulder hung a clean gunny-sack with interesting bulges and bumps. He slung it onto the floor beside the tree, asking if anyone present could read because he had names on the gifts but had forgotten his specs. Many eager voices claimed the ability to read. Finally Maureen and Phoebe were chosen to help Miss Jorgensdatter read names and distribute packages. Sometimes, when they could not be sure, they would hold up the package for all to see and a helpful voice from the rear would call out a name. The surprised person would come forward to receive and exhibit. Sean Moore came forward first, looking somewhat suspicious.

"Sean, me boy," Santa Claus said, "it has come to my attention that ye're a bit in the habit of bein' late—always behind like the old cow's tail." Santa whisked out a cow's-tail brush and handed it to Sean. The audience roared with laughter, and Sean grinned.

"Johnny Martin"—Gopher's older bachelor brother, whose father complained that he spent all his time riding to see his girl, who was reluctant to get married. "Johnny, if she's so stubborn she won't have ye, give 'er the gate!" Santa handed Johnny a small, old picket gate. Again there were appreciative roars of laughter.

Mr. Osborne, who drank too much at times, got a blotter.

Mr. Dawson, who was known to disapprove of tobacco in all forms, received a dented but highly polished spittoon.

Delia Taylor, the old-maid aunt who lived with the Dienstetters, unwrapped a set of harness snaps labeled "useful for traveling in double harness."

There were others. Then Santa began to find presents for the schoolchildren and their little brothers and sisters. By the time the sack was empty and the tree stripped, every child had at least one gift—a jack knife or a bag of marbles, a hand-sewn horsehide ball, a rag or a corn-husk doll, a hand-carved rolling pin, a doll cradle, a jumping rope with carved, fitted wooden handles, a carved wooden boat with real canvas sails to sail on the horse tank—the treasures seemed endless. Hartley and Phoebe got hand-plaited riding whips. Laddie joked to Phoebe that now she could be the teacher for real.

Most of the identified gifts came from children's families, but gifts from Santa Claus also went to families who would have been embarrassed to accept gifts when they could not give in return. Newer families and those who suffered most from the grasshoppers and the drought the year before found themselves with hand-knitted mittens, scarves, socks, and caps. There were also smoked hams, bushels of potatoes, dried apples, and sand plums. There was a wool-filled comfort and a pieced quilt for the Dienstetter family and baby clothes for the Carters, who were expecting their first.

Wade received a package of Brady prints of the Civil War, and looked at the teacher instead of Santa Claus. The teacher smiled across the children milling between them and held up the intricately whittled set of balls within squares that she had unwrapped. Wade walked away.

The gifts went on: butter wrapped in muslin, "Dutch cheese," pickles, jam, preserves. Mrs. Dawson, who had seemed to know about many of the gifts, was genuinely surprised to receive a large package wrapped in a new gunny sack. In it she found a beautiful web of carpet. She thanked Kathleen instead of Santa, and she thanked Mrs. Moore, too.

The older girls worked their way through the packed room to distribute a popcorn ball, a doughnut, molasses cookies, molasses taffy, honey taffy and an orange to everyone present.

Eventually the smaller children began to get sleepy and fretful and parents began to gather their families together. Men started outside to untie their teams.

Wade called above the hubbub, "Quiet, everyone. Teacher has something else to say."

The room came to attention; even the smallest children quieted as the teacher spoke.

"Before we leave, friends, I am happy to present one more present—a present Santa did not know about—to the entire school of Freedom District. The note enclosed with it says, 'A very Merry Christmas to all my young friends of Freedom School, who taught me more, I am sure, than I taught them. Your once-upon-a-time schoolmaster, Elliot Sheldon Gould.'"

A new wave of excitement swept the room. Hartley and Bart, Pat and Mike, Laddie and Kurt, Rube Pfitzer and Alfred came down the aisle in pairs, each carrying a heavy box.

The boys arranged their loads in the front of the room. Wade pulled out his hunting knife from its sheath to pry open lids while voices called, "Careful! Don't cut anything!" The boys and girls, crowding to the front, gasped as the packing was removed.

"Books!" they exclaimed.

"Whillakers! Look at the books!"

"All kinds of colors!"

"Look at the gold!"

Wade handed two to the teacher. As the children started to reach for others, he ordered, "Keep away! You got popcorn sticky on your hands. These are new books, and they're for the whole school. Don't bother them until Miss Jorgensdatter says."

Some of the parents quietly called each other's attention to how the children obeyed Wade without any back talk.

Mr. Lancey allowed himself to be congratulated on what a fine young man his son was, and Mr. Lancey allowed as how it came from proper lickin's when needed.

Miss Jorgensdatter held up the books in her hands for all to see, leafing through one so that the audience could see that there were pictures.

"Wade is right, children. These are beautiful, beautiful new books. You will want to keep them nice. Here is that good story I told you about, *Hans Brinker*, and here is one about plants, and one about animals, and the stars, and *The Illiad* ..."

"That's old A-kill-eze!" Hartley shouted happily.

"Yes! And here are fairy tales, Miss Alcott's books, Aesop ..." She read titles as Wade handed them to her.

"Oh, there are so many wonderful stories you will love. But it is late tonight. We will put them back into the boxes and have a wonderful treasure hunt to look forward to when school starts again after New Year's. And so—shall we finish with a song?"

She did not wait for an answer, but slipped onto the organ bench and began, "Hark! The Herald Angels Sing!"

All joined in. Requests followed for "It Came Upon a Midnight Clear" and then "Oh Tannenbaum," which she began to sing in German. At once, with a radiant smile, Mrs. Pfitzer took it up, her voice rich and full like the big bell. Mr. Pfitzer and all the Dienstetters joined in and the English singers gradually stopped singing to listen.

Softly, the teacher then began, "Silent Night."

The whole room sang, both in German and English, with a lingering, "sleep in heavenly peace."

"Schlaf in himmlischer ruh."

Wagons then were brought to the door. They creaked and rattled their way out of the schoolyard, and excited but tired voices continued to sing. Gradually the sounds of heavenly peace floated away and echoed in the distance as families returned to their isolated homesteads.

Once again the schoolhouse stood silent and empty in the midst of its prairie acres.

CHAPTER EIGHT

WADE SAVES THE DAY

JANUARY AND FEBRUARY passed in such dependable routine that it began to seem as though Freedom School had gone on as it did forever, and forever it would continue unchanged.

The new books were covered with muslin or wrapping paper. Hands were washed ritually before touching them but touched they were, and read and re-read.

Mr. Pfitzer made a beautiful bookcase for them. Its wooden fronts sat on hinges that slid back into the case to make picking out a book easy but dropped down for tight-fitting protection from dust storms.

Mrs. Moore had drawn on the case designs of windmills with curlicues and cornucopias with books pouring out. There were cupids, giants, angels, gophers and prairie dogs, kittens, chickens, buffalo, coyotes and rattlesnakes—all reading.

Wade whittled four little statues to be glued onto the corners. The others carefully carved out the patterns Mrs. Moore traced on the smooth sides and fronts of the case. It was made of black walnut from the Stephenson's grove, rough cut by them and planed by Mr. Pfitzer and his boys. It was a fitting treasure holder for the wonderful books. When children took them home, many parents read the books before they went back. A new book was a rarity in the whole area. No one knew of any school that had a whole caseful.

Wade had been so different since the day of the showdown that it was as if a new scholar had entered school.

When they elected officers and Laddie nominated Wade for mayor as a joke, the other scholars, except Phoebe, Maureen and Tessie, thought he was right for the job. When he was around he was always the leader, so they elected him.

The teacher did not protest—she said anyone could run for office, everyone could vote, and the majority would rule.

Wade took the job seriously with no joking at all. After the Christmas program it was generally said around the blacksmith's forge on the Newton Road, where the men often met, that young Lancey seemed to have sowed his wild oats and was becoming a good citizen. One thing they all agreed on—that Swede girl sure could keep school!

Maureen's reading improved. Her brothers also were able to enjoy easy books, and they all were teaching Kathleen at home at night.

The teacher still taught Maureen and Wade separately, but Wade was ahead of Maureen. He came early, stayed in for most recesses, worked at noon and often stayed after school for extra help. He rode his own horse now so the others did not have to wait for him. If anyone commented he only said "Time's runnin' out for me." Wade would be twenty-one in the summer.

His brothers reported, "Wade and Pa had it out. Pa wants Wade should stop school to plow. Wade said he won't, because after he's of age this summer he can't never go to school no more but he can plow all the rest of his born days. Pa said he'd lick him and Wade didn't even fight. He just laughed and said, "I reckon not. But I been thinking what I'll do is write a paper that I owe you six months work, for now until I'm twenty-one, and I'll pay it next year before I get married and homestead for myself."

"And Pa shut up and took it!"

"Married? Who's Wade going to marry?"

"Who knows? Pro'bly Wade don't. For a while last fall we thought he was sweet on Kathleen, but she wouldn't give him the time of day. Now seems like he's got book learnin' in his craw."

So the others let him alone to work. Most of the time he did so with his chin resting in his hands, his elbows on his desk and a frown on his face; even Laddie finally gave up on pestering him.

March came. Warm winds blew, the sun shone, and the tall prairie grass waved like a rippling ocean. Winter wheat was green, cattle contentedly ate themselves toward slaughtering time, and soon the spring work would pile up on everyone.

At Freedom School the children continued to learn. In the morning every scholar worked on his own unfinished lessons for the week while Miss Jorgensdatter helped children one by one. Anyone whose work was complete could plan for himself, and many worked in little groups, practicing songs, drilling each other on spelling or times tables, rehearsing their memory pieces or practicing penmanship while one of them read to the others.

Fridays were special at the school. At noon they all put their lunches together; they set up the boards on the sawhorses to make a long table, spread out clean red-checked or blue-checked tablecloths, which volunteers brought from home, and every scholar brought a plate, knife, fork and spoon. And a napkin. Even if it was just a clean rag everyone had a neat, folded napkin beside his neatly arranged place. When the teacher gave the signal, everyone washed his hands carefully and waited quietly until all were ready. The hostess for the day would then announced, "Dinner is served."

The littlest children took their turns with the rest. Seats were pushed around to make room for as many as possible;

the rest took turns on different days at their own desks, but all pretended they were "seated polite." The first few weeks there had been much pushing, shoving, giggling and objection, especially from the boys to the rule that the girls should be seated first. But the teacher insisted.

"If you know all your other lessons, but have bad manners, people you meet will think you are ignorant hayseeds. After you learn how to eat politely, if you don't want to do it that is your choice. But you have no freedom of choice if you don't know how to do it right."

Somehow polite eating on Fridays settled into a game and then a habit.

During the meal, everyone was supposed to talk, not with a mouthful, and then to listen. "Conversation is an important skill and listening is an important part of it," the teacher explained.

During the week the older ones read the copies of papers and magazines the teacher brought so they could report something interesting for dinner conversation. The little ones were encouraged to notice and tell about what was going on around them. Today there were reports of new lambs, new colts, tumbleweeds and sunflowers above ground, spring cleaning and carpet beating, windmill repairs, returning meadowlarks and bob-whites.

Maureen announced, "Jessie Deacon and Alonzo Carter got married in El Dorado."

"Who are they?"

"I don't know, but they got married in the *Wichita Eagle*."

Tessie waited politely to tell about her exciting find.

"At Colton School in Sedgwick County, a little boy chased a butterfly and got lost in the prairie grass. They hunted and hunted, and it was getting dark, and they thought maybe a rattlesnake had bit him. Then his big brother climbed on top of the schoolhouse and way off he saw the grass moving against the wind. He called to the others and someone rode while he pointed and yelled where to go, and there was the little boy all safe."

Another child then took his turn sharing news. "A big prairie fire twenty miles wide burned in McPherson County all day. It was so hot two women were burned to death from the hot air where the fire didn't even burn the buildings."

"I read that too," Tessie said excitedly. "Where the barn stood nothing was left but the buckles and things from the harnesses. Even the leather was burned."

Uneasily the children looked out the windows at the waving, tall grass blowing in steady ripples beyond the plowed ground firebreak around the schoolyard.

"Father plowed two more rows on our firebreak last week," a Dienstetter added. "Now it's as big as the one here at school."

Miss Jorgensdatter said calmly, "We are protected here. The creek is on the west, and if a fire is reported from another direction men will ride to spread the alarm and ring the farm bells. If necessary we would ride off in another direction."

"Twisters is what you can't watch out for. Over White-water way a twister took a house right up in the air," one wide-eyed scholar warned.

Maureen, buttering bread for Ellen, said cheerfully, "A good thing about a sod house like ours is that no prairie fire or twister would even know it was there. It is all thick sod and can't burn, and it's so tight a part of the earth itself that the wind has nothing to take hold of."

"If the crops are good and the grasshoppers don't come back, we're going to have a frame house next fall, Pa said. Not so big as the Dawsons', but real wood just the same," Anton Kavel said proudly.

In the afternoon was the program. Everyone had a part. There were recitations and poems and songs as at Christmas. But there also were times-tables contests and contests to find places on the map.

Today there was to be a play that the older scholars had made from the story of Achilles. Phoebe had a solo on the organ, and their teacher would accompany her on the violin. All the children had combs with paper over them to make a band to play "Yankee Doodle," Mike thumped a real tom-tom he had made with steer hide stretched over a hollowed-out log, and Tessie banged two tin plates together in time with him.

Lastly came the spelling contest.

"Friday afternoons are great," Sean spoke for all of them, "because then we don't have any lessons."

In February there were usually visitors, but with spring work starting up no patrons were expected to take time off. Still, there were now forty-two scholars, who made a critical audience. All performers struggled with nervousness and eagerness to win the contests.

The play was applauded. Kurt won the mental arithmetic contest to Hartley's chagrin. Tessie was racing nervously through a memorized piece by Mr. Bronson Alcott called "Heavenly Vegetables," when the quiet audience was startled.

Wade, who as mayor had been sitting in front presiding, suddenly jumped up and almost ran to the window, not even trying to walk softly.

Tessie stopped. All eyes turned to Wade, but he only looked out then turned and ran out the back door.

The scholars looked to the teacher. She too looked startled for once but quickly turned on her calm smile and said, "Go on, Tessie."

"I forget where I was."

"Then begin again at the beginning and take it slower."

Obediently Tessie started again, and the others shrugged and settled back courteously. Tessie was almost through this time when Wade ran back in.

"Listen everyone!" his voice was sharp.

"Get into two lines. Start with the oldest on this side— you, Maureen, Mike, Pat, Phoebe—and the littlest across from them—Ellen, Abe, Anton, Dennie, David—fast."

Almost automatically they started to obey, then caught themselves and looked at Miss Jorgensdatter. For once she was at a loss for words.

"Wade?" she questioned.

He turned to her. "Kirsten, we've got to get them to the creek fast. The whole west is on fire and the wind has shifted and it's coming this way. We've got to beat the fire to the creek."

"But if it is the other side of the creek ..."

"It will cross the creek—too fast to run away from. Smoldering cornstalks already are blowing in the wind and falling on this side; the black smoke is rolling this way. We'll smell it in a few minutes. Hurry!"

Turning back to the children, he went on, "Hartley, go ring that bell as long as you can see us. Then catch up with me."

Hartley darted out. Phoebe and Maureen were getting the lines in order; some of the children began whimpering and clinging to the older girls. Hepzibah ducked under a desk, but most of them were in place.

Wade ordered, "Each big one hold the hand of a little one and don't let go! Stay together!

"Kirsten, you and Mike go ahead. When you get to the creek separate and lead up and downstream so's there's room for everyone.

"Big ones, walk fast and don't fall; little ones, hold on and run enough to keep up. When you get to the creek, dig in. Keep all your clothes on. Cover yourselves with mud as thick as you can, get your hair good, and your faces; then lie on your bellies with just your nose out of water and breathe right down by the top of the water. And stay there! Big ones, see the kids are fixed and hold their hands.

"Don't anyone get scared and raise up. The fire will cross the creek in the treetops, I think. It will be awful hot and make a lot of noise, so be ready and keep down! Don't anyone raise up. Kirsten, give me your hand bell. Everyone, I'll ring the little bell when you can raise up. March!"

With a final look at Wade the teacher moved to the front of the line.

"Come, children," she said quietly.

In spite of the excitement, Phoebe noticed that look. She realized it was the kind of look she had seen between her mother and father!

Wade gripped the teacher's hand and said softly, "Go fast but don't fall. And for God's sake, pray, Kirsten. I think we are all right if we make the creek before the flames do!"

He called her Kirsten and she didn't even look surprised. She just nodded, picked up the reluctant Hepzibah and carried her, big as she was, through the door at the fast walk Wade had ordered.

As they turned west around the building toward the creek, they slowed. The fierce, scorching wind hit them; they had to lean against it. Now they could see the boiling black air, and a burning cornstalk sailing here and there. The smoke thickened the air.

"My eyes hurt!" someone whimpered.

"Move!" Wade shouted. "Walk fast!"

They were all trying not to run, blinking and stumbling on rocks and clods as the teacher led the way down the plowed firebreak ground. If one of those blazing torches from the sky fell on it, there was less danger than in the hedgerow or on the open grass.

The clanging school bell mingled its alarm with the growing roar from the west. Phoebe prayed that Hartley did not stay too long. Once the smoke closed in he could get lost—but she must keep up with the line. She rubbed her eyes and gripped little Dennie Dienstetter's hand harder.

She felt a tug on her dress skirt followed by a command, "Pass it on. Everyone hold on in front."

A million miles of rough ground lie ahead, then came the end of the firebreak and a frightening piece of tall prairie grass. Somehow finally the trees of the creek bank loomed as darker shadows in the shadowy air, and Laddie and Pat, standing at the creek edge, helped Phoebe and her charge down the bank. Mike grabbed her hand and pulled her farther downstream as she heard Bart helping Maureen and Ellen ahead of her upstream.

"Now duck!" Wade yelled.

The air was getting very hot; the water felt good. Phoebe frantically dug fistfuls of mud, plastered it on Dennie's hair and pushed him into a shallow pool at the edge of the bank where no trees hung over. She sat beside him, water over her legs, still digging mud and plastering herself. When she finished she lay on her stomach close to Dennie.

"Keep still, Dennie," she repeated, "that's a brave little man."

All the while she was trying not to wonder where Tessie, David, Robbie and Hartley were. She realized she no longer heard the big bell. Was it the roar of the fire? Had Hartley left in time? And what of their family at home?

Suddenly Phoebe realized she had raised up, starting to run back to look for the others. "Down!" she yelled at herself.

"I'm down!" several voices answered.

There were voices and calls, then a big splashing nearby. The air was thick now; it was hard to breathe and she wanted to look. She put her hand on Dennie's head then heard Wade's voice, "How many from your end?"

"Twenty-six," Mike answered.

"Forty-four take away twenty-six is eighteen, ain't it?"

"Yeah."

"We got sixteen above. Two are missing. I think it's Phoebe and Dennie."

"We're right over here at the side, Wade!"

"Then we're all here."

The roar was growing louder; things began dropping into the water here and there and sizzling; a crackling began to add to the roar. Footsteps splashed and Wade's voice, near but moving, yelled, "Down everyone. Down, down down!"

Phoebe felt Dennie's fingers jerk in hers, and she held them tight, the mud squishing under them. Sideways she could see he was breathing as directed, his nose almost touching the water.

The roar grew; the crackling was now all around them. The oven door was open.

Phoebe thought to herself, "And the gates of hell shall not prevail against thee ... He leadeth me beside the still waters ... The Lord is my shepherd ... Thine is the power and the glory ... Thy will be done ..."

Time seemed endless; breathing hurt. It seemed as though days went by, although she knew it could only have been a few minutes. Dennie coughed and choked, but then breathed again smoothly. Phoebe heard more coughing, but no voices. The air seemed thinner. She desperately wanted to raise up and look, but instead she held Dennie tighter. The mud smelled funny. She got too close and got some in her mouth, but it felt good.

At last! The stillness began to grow as the roar moved off toward the east. With coughing up and down the stream increasing, there came the unmistakable ring of the bell.

The signal! They could get up!

Dennie, slick with mud, crawled into her arms. She could hear voices now and more crying. The wind, which had brought the fire so fast, now was blowing it away fast. From the north came uneven little gusts bringing gasps of clear air. The darkness was getting lighter; they could see each other and the creek banks!

Unbelievable! The world they had left was gone.

The graceful, drooping cottonwoods, leaning their branches out over the stream, were blackened and smoldering. At the foot of the bank where Phoebe had scooped mud the ground was now dry, showing her fingerprints like baked mud pies. Phoebe quickly realized she was not hurt.

"Are you all right, Dennie?"

"I'm hungry!" he said surprisingly.

"Good. Thank you God, oh thank you, and please let the rest be safe!"

By now the children in all directions were scrambling, calling, crying, and splashing. Beyond the rise of the bank they could see the scarlet flames billowing in gusts into the boiling black and white smoke. As the fire moved east the children gripped each other and watched, paralyzed. The flames swirled higher, seeming to circle.

"Will it come back?" a frightened voice asked.

"No," the teacher's familiar, calm voice assured. "There is nothing here to burn."

The gusts of clear air suddenly became a steady, strong wind from the north. The circle of flames changed direction, moving toward the south ahead of the wind. Gradually the fire's light dimmed; smoke still rolled off the prairie to the southeast but seemed lower, and no longer moving much.

Near Phoebe, Hartley's voice sounded clear. "I think it has reached the Nelson's wheat. There's a hundred acres of green, and then an eighty of fall-plowed corn. Maybe it will die out."

"Hartley," Phoebe called in relief, "are you all right?"

"Yes. So are Tessie and the boys."

"And the others?"

"Some got a lot of smoke, but no one seems bad."

Just then Wade's voice, husky but loud, ordered, "Stay in the middle of the creek and start walking upstream till we get out of the path."

It was a relief to be moving, even with soggy shoes and heavy, wet clothes. Again they were leaning against the wind, which was becoming cold. They began to shiver.

Despite the chill, they were relieved to be breathing air rather than smoke. There was some crying but few complaints as they slogged along one squishy step at a time. Everyone continued to hold onto each other as they stepped across the slippery rocks.

The teacher's voice now was directing. "Come along. A little farther, hold your partners."

The big boys began carrying some of the littlest, taking them upstream a ways, then going back for other laggards.

Laddie laughed. "Just like a cattle drive, huh, Wade? Always having to wagon-back and carry the calves a while!"

But there was not much talking; they needed their breath for walking. Hearing David's voice behind her, Phoebe slowed to take him with her free hand while Alfred left them to help others. Here and there they saw rabbits, mice, gophers and squirrels sharing the creek refuge. Some were drowned, some were swimming and scrambling frantically. A hawk with feathers burned nearly off had dropped on a mud bank. The children slogged forward: splash, squish, slurp.

Suddenly a jubilant cry rang out up ahead, "The Pfitzer's plowed ground!"

"And the trees aren't black. We are there!"

They began to break ranks, running, slipping and falling but helping each other up again. Everyone scrambled up the fairly steep bank to throw themselves in relief on the good, hard, rough dry clods.

Like good stock dogs, the leaders rounded up the children, gathering everyone finally into a large circle.

"Count off!" the teacher called.

Once more everyone was there!

Suddenly, right in front of everyone, Miss Jorgensdatter turned to Wade, who was standing behind her, threw her arms around his neck and cried. Wade held her tight, patting her mud-caked hair as he hoarsely repeated, "It's all over, dear. Don't cry. It's all over."

No one paid much attention. They were busy thinking of themselves and their families.

"Oh, Hartley, I've been trying not to think. Are they all right, do you suppose?"

"Doesn't look like it burned any settled part except the school. The wind shifted in time, but they will worry."

"Oh, Hartley, do run!"

Hartley was tugging at his mud-caked, soaked boot lacings. "Help me get these off. They hurt my feet, and I can make it better barefoot."

They could not get the wet leather thongs to let go until Tessie came with a borrowed pocketknife. The laces cut, Hartley and Phoebe each pulled off a boot, and he ran. The children watched him hopping gingerly from one furrow to another until he disappeared in the smoky shadows that still hovered.

"Papa will come now!" a voice spoke out confidently.

All their spirits rose. They walked a little faster to fight the cold, looking, listening, expecting any moment to see horses, men or the Dienstetter wagon.

Nothing. Time passed. The children, exhausted already, lost their new push and began to droop. The wind was hard against them and getting colder by the minute. It seemed a long, long time before they heard, not the noise of horses and wagon, but a bell pealing far off to the northeast.

"It's the Dawsons' bell," someone said knowingly. The clangs sounded sometimes very near, then far, far away.

"Wind gusts!" Gopher shouted.

The little ones could go no further, and the older boys were tired, too. Wade was coughing hard.

"We will wait here," the teacher's voice called. "Get as close together as you can everyone. Put the littlest in the middle and we will all sit with our backs to the wind in turn."

"Like the cows do?"

"Yes, like the cows do."

Huddled together, a little warmer, they felt how good it was not to have to move or think. The bell tones still called in fitful gusts. Help would come. All they needed to do now was wait.

Some of the children whimpered softly. But except for some coughing and sneezing here and there they were fairly quiet. To the south the air was smoky, but no more flames lighted the clearing sky.

In the stillness the teacher's voice, low and clear, came to them, "I will give thanks to the Lord with my whole heart."

Maureen, who had been crooning softly to her little sisters, said out loud, "Blessed art thou, Mary, and the fruit of thy womb, Jesus."

Gus's voice was deep, "A mighty fortress is our God."

Others joined in, remembering words they had memorized because someone made them, now understanding why.

"O Lord, my God, in thee do I put my trust."

"I will sing unto the Lord because he hath dealt bountifully with me."

"The fool hath said in his heart, 'There is no God.'"

"God is love!"

"I am poured out like water and all my bones are out of joint; my heart is like wax."

"He shall cover thee with his feathers, and under his wings shalt thou trust."

Suddenly several people saw a wagon moving from the northeast.

"It's Mother!" Robbie screamed.

With new life they surged around her as she pulled up the horses and jumped down.

"Hartley thought you were all safe?" her voice questioned. She dared not believe.

The teacher clung to Mrs. Dawson's shawl.

"The children seem all right. They are wet and cold but safe. I'm so glad to have someone else responsible."

For the second time that day, her voice broke. Mrs. Dawson reached one arm past Tessie and patted the teacher. Then she felt and hugged everyone within reach.

"Mrs. Dawson," the teacher said, "Wade is sick. He was slightly burned, and I'm afraid he inhaled too much smoke."

Quickly Mrs. Dawson turned to Wade, doubled on the ground.

"Wade, can you get into the wagon? Boys, help him in and put in as many of the little ones as you can. There's straw and some sheepskins to warm them. Take out that pile of comforts and blankets and the bearskins and buffalo robes—the rest of you cover up the best you can with them. Someone else will get here soon. No one was home at the Pfitzers because they had all gone to fight the fire. I left Hartley at home with the babies. He will tell the men where to come. They will have heard the bell and we'll soon have you all snug. I'll take these on to the Pfitzers, it's closest."

The heartbreaking worry she had been through hardly showed as she helped pack in one more child. With words of encouragement for the others she climbed up again and urged the horses to their fastest trot.

"If they're all night coming, I guess I could stand it," Laddie said as she drove out. "It feels like a huge grindstone is gone, not needing to worry about the children."

Before they had pulled the robes around themselves they saw more movement. Soon they heard the voices of Mr. Pfitzer, Mr. and Mrs. Moore, and a blur of others mingling with the rumble of wagons and the heavy beat of trotting horses.

Phoebe found herself held tightly in her father's arm, while Tessie clung around his neck. As he clung to his daughters he repeated again and again, "Thank you, God, thank you, God, oh, thank you, thank you, God."

Phoebe sobbed softly, "Amen."

CHAPTER NINE

THE WAKE AND THE NEW DREAM

*I*T WAS LATE when the last tub of muddy water was emptied. Wet heads were rubbed and dried by the stoves, everyone was fed, and the five exhausted Dawson school-children were tucked into clean, dry beds. They slept late, waking to the roar of a cold March storm whistling down the chimneys and carrying flakes of snow. Their mother feared pneumonia and wanted them to stay in bed. Once they were allowed to pack into the boys' bedroom together they were content to rest and talk. They took turns holding the baby, Louisa May, while Martha and Mary Ann crawled and scrambled over them, helping them rest. Like a litter of puppies they all wanted to be close to push away the memories and fears. Mrs. Dawson hovered, touching them, feeling for fever, singing little bits of hymns and then breaking off and leaving the room, only to return in a few minutes and do it all over.

Mr. Dawson was in often, patting heads, letting the children talk to soothe themselves and him. He ignored the pressures of the spring work.

After dinner Mrs. Dawson insisted on a real nap for the children. Their father borrowed Pal to ride around to check on the neighbors.

He returned with news.

"They drove Wade to the doctor's in Newton last night. He has some burns on his hands and face. He inhaled quite a bit of smoke and his eyes are irritated, but the doctor thinks he will be all right before very long.

"The doctor reported the whole thing to the man from the *Wichita Eagle*. He sent it out on the wires, so you all are in the eastern papers today! What do you think of that?"

Such excitement was hard to deal with. Tessie said, "I never thought of real people being in the papers."

Phoebe added, "Minnie Masterson was in the *Wichita Eagle*, but I guess she never was in the eastern papers."

Suddenly they were all tired of bed and were permitted to get up for supper. Phoebe offered to wash dishes, but for once Mrs. Dawson insisted on stacking them until morning. Instead, the whole family gathered around the stove. The little boys were on their father's lap; Tessie held baby Louisa May, cuddling close to her mother in the big chair; and Phoebe and Hartley sat on the floor, leaning against their parents' legs, each holding one of the little girls. It was good to be home, and safe and close.

They did not talk about their adventure any more. They told riddles and stories and sang fun songs. While the family relaxed together Mr. Dawson quietly joined David and Robbie's hands, reaching his other hand down to Hartley. Hartley in turn held Martha's. As the circle of hands was completed Mr. Dawson began singing out strongly, "Now, thank we all our God."

Even the little girls made singing noises. Only Louisa May was quiet.

As they finished Mr. Dawson said, "God, you know how grateful we all are that our circle is still complete. Let us never forget how rich you have made us, and how safe we are with you, whatever happens. Comfort those in the world tonight who are suffering what we have not had to suffer. And help us all use the lives you have given us to serve others who need us and you. Amen."

"Amen" was echoed around the circle. That night even David slept without nightmares.

Sunday morning the wind was gone. The fickle weather had changed again to bright, still sunshine. The windows were opened and sweet-smelling breezes drifted through the house.

The Moore wagon packed with the entire family rumbled into the yard with Laddie Kavel on horseback beside them.

"We've come for dinner!" they all shouted.

The women unpacked hampers and tubs of food while the men and boys took the team to the barn and the children clustered in chattering groups. Mrs. Moore explained their arrival. "I've never seen the children so down. They've been tormenting us to go look at where the school was and they wanted yours with them. Maureen, big as she is, cried and said she wants to go and say "good-bye." I don't know your feelings, Marian, but I think there's some peace of mind in a wake, maybe for a place as much as for a person. So I said we'd bring our dinners and eat with you. Laddie just happened to be by, so we brought him, too. If you and Francis don't mind, and yours want to go, let them all go over together and see for themselves."

"I don't know myself what is left," Mrs. Dawson admitted. "Francis hasn't mentioned it, and I have had other things on my mind, and I didn't like to bring it up."

"Nothing's left! Not a thing at all! And when I think ..." Mrs. Moore bit her lip. Both women held each other and cried. Seeing their mothers crying, both families of little ones were frightened and began to cry. The women laughed through their tears, wiped their eyes on their aprons, and comforted their children before sending them out to play. Everyone comforted themselves with the familiar ritual of Sunday dinner. They talked over their hours of worry.

"It all seemed to happen at once, like a nightmare," Mrs. Dawson remembered. "When I heard the sudden ringing of the school bell gone mad I ran out and saw the smoke in the west and began to smell it. I grabbed the babies and got them into the old soddy for safety even though I didn't think the fire could get this far. Francis rode in; he unhitched the plow and rode Dan back. He just yelled, 'the school' and was gone.

"I dared not let myself believe that the fire could jump the creek. I watched and watched while the palominos raced into the corral, snorting and laying their ears back. Old Captain came next—he's not been himself since."

"Great it was of Hartley to let all the horses loose before he ran. He's a boy to be proud of."

"They're all to be proud of—all those children! And that Wade Lancey—who ever would have thought?"

"From what I hear, it's not just book lessons made a man of Wade," Ellen Moore laughed. "Well, I'm hoping they'll homestead near here. She'll be a good neighbor to have."

As the women talked the young people crowded around to eat. The Dawsons were eager to go.

"I've been dreading seeing it again," Phoebe said. "It will be better seeing it together. That way we all can get it over with."

When everyone was full of chicken and dumplings and custard pie and all the rest they swarmed to climb into the Moore wagon. Then they decided to take both wagons and go around for the Pfitzers and Martins. Finally it was decided that Larry and Hartley, with Pat on Star, would ride on to the more distant families while Maureen and Mike drove the two wagons for the closer ones.

"Seems like they yearn to be together," Mrs. Moore said.

"Like veterans of a battle," Mr. Moore agreed. "'twill be better after they see the place and can comfort each other."

"Maureen and the boys asked if there was any chance of rebuilding."

"Of course. But I don't know when. The district is taxed to the limit to pay for the other one. Don't see how we can spend more until most of those bills are paid. Maybe in another year the state can help."

"It's a sad thing for the older ones just getting their first chance."

The four sat in silence.

The wagons pulled up at the edge of the schoolyard and the children sat in silence. They just looked, remembering, trying to believe what they saw.

The schoolyard itself, its cut grass trampled by playing children all winter, looked normal. But the lovely white building had vanished; the neat lines of a black rectangle of ground enclosed its ashes. Charred pieces of wood and unidentifiable rubble lie within the stone foundation posts. Smoke-blackened sod slabs that were the base of the shed outlined where it had stood. In front, in its own pile of burned ashes, the beautiful bell lay on its side. As Hartley, the Dienstetters and the Martins rode up, Mike swung down and walked to the bell. He lifted it by the hole for the rope and swung it once to let the clapper hit. It gave forth a dull thud. Mike threw it down and turned away from the others, his hand over his face.

"Well," Tessie said at last with a little choke, "at least we won't have to paint those hedge-apple stains!"

Maureen and Phoebe broke into tears, and most of the rest joined them.

The boys tried to hide their faces. They began to shuffle through the rubble, calling to each other, "Look! Here's the metal braces from the desks all over."

"And lunch pails and the nails they hung on all in a row."

"The stove."

"The water bucket!"

"The wire that held the curtains for the plays."

"And cracked window glass everywhere."

The girls joined them. Holding hands, they turned over strange objects with their feet, careless of the soot and ashes.

163

Suddenly Phoebe stooped over, crying, "Look! Here's where the bookcase was. The books are lying in a pile and you can still read some of the pages."

She brushed off the charred outside of one. "Robinson Crusoe!"

Others joined her. At the bottom of the solid heap they found a number of books that were merely scorched. They began brushing off the black, arranging the remains on a pile on the cleaner ground outside of the cornerstones.

Spotting something shiny, Gopher Martin called, "Here's the brass plate from the organ."

But nothing else could they find of it except some browned ivory keys and some screws.

"The teacher's violin was on top."

"There's nothing left of it."

"We never got to hear her duet with you, Phoebe."

"Do you suppose she's going to marry Wade?"

"They sure acted like they knew each other better than just in school."

"No wonder he's been staying after so much for help!"

"Wasn't old Wade wonderful the way he knew what to do, and making us stay down and staying up too long himself."

"And now we are in the papers Back East—can you believe it?"

Maureen sighed. "Wade was learning to read real well. Now by the time we can have a school again, he and I will be over twenty-one."

"I can teach you, Maureen," Laddie said.

"Well, it looks like old Wade won't stop for any birthday. Bart says the teacher's been staying in Newton so she can see him every single day at the doctor's house where he's staying."

Ellen, her dress front dirtied by a blackened book that she was clutching, pushed in-between the older ones.

"Sister, here's that nice story about Red Riding Hood. The pretty cover is hardly burned. Read me it."

Maureen sadly kissed her and handed the book to Phoebe.

Other younger ones gathered around and begged and Phoebe, seated on the ground, began to read to them. Soon the wind shifted, and although the sun was warm the breeze was sharp.

"Let's get behind the shed," the children suggested. They swarmed to huddle in the sunshine, protected by the remaining sod walls. But the walls were not high enough to protect the bigger girls, or long enough for all who wanted to join.

"I wish we could cut some more sod," Tessie exclaimed, "and build us a little playhouse. We could play school, and you could read to us and we could say our timeses and play it was real school."

"And we could have maps on the ground, like we did with Mr. Gould," David spoke up for the first time.

"And we could have our museum again. This is the time to find things like bugs, baby rattlesnakes, and birds' nests."

"We couldn't write," Robbie moaned.

For an answer, Hartley motioned to Pat and Mike, who were interested in the children's talk. The three boys lifted off the top layer of blackened rock from the foundation pile, uncovering the hardly smudged pale-green limestone underneath. With growing excitement Hartley searched for a moment among the ashes. When he found what he wanted, a charred small piece of wood, he began marking on the rock.

"Remember Mr. Gould told us about people before they had slates and pencils. They used burned wood and made pictures and signs on rocks."

"Jesus wrote with his staff on the ground and then rubbed it out, probably with his shoe. We could do that, too." Laddie suggested.

"We could sing."

"And play on combs and paper."

"I could easily make another tom-tom."

Maureen stood, laughing sadly. "Enough daydreaming. It's getting chilly. We must be getting back."

Ellen pulled loose from Kathleen and ran to grab the hands of her two big brothers.

"But if we had a sod playhouse to keep out the wind, we could come back and have all that fun. We'd have stories, and count things ... Please Pat and Mike, won't you please help us—like you and Father made our nice house at home?"

Pat laughed, but Mike picked her up and answered her seriously.

"It's maybe more work than you think, Mavourneen. And spring work is behind already. It doesn't take so long to build a small soddy; it took two days for ours at home, but we sold the sod-cutter plow. Cutting sod by hand would take too much time away from the fields."

He seemed to be talking to himself. Gus suddenly spoke up.

"Like they was saying, it would be a place we could ride over and do something when work was done. Like Sundays—and after harvest. A Mennonite man named Chris Muller, behind Newton, he's a friend of ours. He's a bachelor who likes children, and he's got a sod-breaker plow. I bet he'd take a day and come cut enough sod for a little place for us. We could lay it up ourselves."

"Once he's set up, he could cut enough sod for a real schoolhouse just as easy as for a little play one, and it would do a lot more good," Hartley said excitedly.

"Where'll we build it?" someone asked, and everyone began to answer at once.

"Let's build it right on the old ground. That's already been leveled, we just need to shovel it off and wash it good. It will have a good, packed floor already," Mike suggested.

Without more talk, Robbie, David and Tessie, then Ellen, Sean and Gopher began to pick up debris from the ruins and carry it outside. The big girls noticed.

"Stop. Look at you! All ashes and soot. Whatever will your mothers say!"

"We just wanted to get started."

Pat interrupted. "What we need is some scoop shovels and something to sweep with. Bunches of wet straw might do it."

"At least we still got the well."

"But when will we do it?" Laddie looked at the older Moores. "With spring planting breathing down our necks ..."

There was a pause. Then Phoebe said, in brisk tones like her mother's, "Let's take a vote. How many want to build a sod schoolhouse?"

Gopher counted the raised hands and announced, "It's anonymous."

"What's that mean?" Irene asked.

"Means everyone wants to."

"I am pretty sure the word you mean is 'unanimous'," Phoebe corrected. "Anyway, if most of the school helped we could do an awful lot in one day. I know tomorrow we all have to work. But if we could get word around and everyone asked if we could have one day for the schoolhouse—maybe Wednesday or Thursday—we could all promise to work harder and faster at home to make up the time."

"But what if Gus's friend won't cut the sod? And where can we get rafter wood to hold the roof? A ridge pole costs a lot."

"Maybe we couldn't finish it."

"One thing is sure," Kathleen said decisively, "we can't finish if we don't start. I'm thinkin' Phoebe has a grand plan, and I'm thinkin' our father and mother would say 'yes'—especially right now when they're still thinkin' of what if everyone was lost."

It was indeed getting chilly now. They knew they must get back, especially if they wanted to ask a big favor.

Quickly they divided up names, agreeing on who was to ride where to spread the word. Gus said he would ask to have his time off the next morning so he could ride to Newton to see Mr. Muller. Then they could get word round again in time if Mr. Muller was not coming. And since each one was just going to ask for one day off, he would make up by giving up working with the others in order to help at home.

The rest of the boys pounded him on the shoulders to show their pleasure. All agreed that whoever could would come Thursday. That would give people more time to get ready and allow enough time to get word to everyone. They could all show at home what they meant by working harder to make up for time they were going to lose.

"Actions speak louder than words," Kathleen reminded them.

"We'll show them—all of them!" Gopher said, which elicited some emphatic "amens."

Great was the Moore and Dawson parents' astonishment when their wagonloads of children returned singing at the tops of their voices from what was supposed to have been a wake for the schoolhouse!

CHAPTER TEN

THE MUSTARD SEED

*T*HE CHILDREN ALL talked at once.

"We're going to build a new schoolhouse right on top of the old one."

"A soddy, like our house, Mama!"

"Everyone is going to teach everyone else what he knows best. Phoebe will teach us to read, and Kurt and Hartley will have arithmetic ..."

"Kathleen's going to teach us weaving—the boys, too—like in the old country, as soon as the Pfitzers get their pa to help build a big loom like Kathleen's little one."

"And Maureen will teach us to cook in the fireplace, and Phoebe will write down receipts for things we cook, and we can learn to read them."

"We're going to get old newspapers that nobody bought, like Miss Jorgensdatter did."

"Most every family has a Bible—we can bring those to read. Whillakers, anyone can learn some real hard reading out of the Bible."

Hartley and Phoebe slowed down first, noticing their father was sadly shaking his head.

"I hate to discourage you children. But can't you see Gus was dreaming. A man with a sod-breaker plow and oxen has money tied up in them. He will have all the work he can handle the way settlers are pouring in. He has to get paid to get his money back, no matter how kind he is.

"Maybe we will hear from the state in the fall. When there's a little let-up after harvest and if crops are good, we'll see. Meanwhile there's all the spring work ..."

Quietly, Ellen began to cry against Kathleen's skirt. Robbie aimlessly scuffled his toes on the floor. Everyone's shoulders drooped.

Then Phoebe asked, "Well if he should say he'll come and cut sod, can we take a day off to work on the schoolhouse? If we all work extra hard to make up at home?"

Mr. Dawson smiled and patted her head.

"Daughter, you have the right spirit for a pioneer. Yes, I think we are safe in saying that if a stranger leaves his work to cut sod for you, you can spend all day helping."

Mr. and Mrs. Moore, smiling, but not looking happy, agreed that it was a safe promise.

"Well," Phoebe said, "remember Christian in *Pilgrim's Progress*? When lions roared up ahead in his way, he kept putting one foot in front of the other instead of running away. When he got there, the lions were chained and he went through safely.

"Mother, you're always saying, 'Nothing succeeds like trying.' So I'm ready to start. What do you want me to do here first?"

Mrs. Dawson's mouth trembled and she kissed Phoebe.

"We will all try, Daughter. We will work and pray and accept. Now I guess the thing for us to do is to get supper."

The older Moore boys offered to ride home and do the milking and other evening chores. Hartley and the younger boys started at a run to get their cows in and do their own chores. Laddie offered to pump water for the girls as they all poured into the kitchen to start supper. Again the four grownups were left in sudden silence.

"Dawson, do you think there is a chance?"

"No. I'm afraid not. But disappointments come to all of us. I guess they will just have to live with it for themselves."

"In a bit they'll be running down," Mrs. Moore added.

But when Mrs. Dawson got up the next morning with the baby before the five o'clock alarm went off, she discovered the table set for breakfast. Mush simmered on the back of the stove and a lantern gleamed from the barn. She called her husband, who dressed quickly and went out.

"Daughter!" he exclaimed, as he found Phoebe already milking.

"We thought we'd better get an early start. I know it's a little early for the cows, but Hartley says they'll give that much more this evening. He's hitching up to plow."

And they kept up. Even Robbie and David worked so hard all morning that David went to sleep in his chair at dinner, prompting Mrs. Dawson to proclaim an hour's rest for all.

But when it was over they started again, a little slower, but steady. By nightfall even they were amazed at how much they had gotten done. They were almost too tired to eat supper but insisted they would do as much the next day.

Phoebe and Tessie were in the kitchen washing dishes before the others finished their meal; they were the first to hear hoofbeats.

Gus burst into the house yelling. "He's coming! He's coming! Old Chris said he is coming Thursday. He's got two more days where he is, then he said the next job can wait a day."

The Dawson children jumped for joy, their tiredness forgotten. Mr. Dawson asked incredulously, "Are you sure, Gus, that the man understood there is no money at all to pay him?"

"Yah. He knows. He says he'll work, God will pay. He says that crackin' open heads and plantin' some knowledge is more important than crackin' open sod to plant some corn any time. He says a country goin' to have people govern demselfes, dey first got to know someting; he don't want to be a old man in a country where dummkopfs grow up to run it. He comes Thursday. Wednesday night he comes to our house, so it starts early."

Gus's horse was at home, "played out." Gus was riding a work horse that he had to get back. According to their earlier plans, Phoebe, instead of dropping into bed, rode Star to pass the word to the Moore's while Hartley went to the Martin's. Each family would "pass it on" until the news was spread. Mr. Dawson called them the "Paul Revere Squad."

Tuesday and Wednesday the children worked more slowly, but with a steadiness that amazed their parents. Thursday morning they rushed through their routine chores, and not long after sunup they pulled out of the yard with a wagonload of supplies to help with the cleanup: old straw, a bucket, a long rope to draw water from the well—they had discovered the pump did not work—a scoop shovel, and a spade. Phoebe asked her mother for two bleached sugar sacks "for something special." She sat holding them and smiling as David curled against her for some more sleep.

Several families arrived about the same time. As the boys took stock of tools and began planning the clean-up, Phoebe gathered the girls at the side of the wagon and showed her white sacks, sewed together lengthwise. And a pail of dried mulberries. She also had a bottle of bluing. Giggling, the girls began hunting through the ashes for pieces of charred wood. The sacks were spread smooth against the wagon sides and the girls went to work.

"Phoebe, make the outside of the letters so they look alike. Then we will fill them in," Kathleen directed.

Soon the girls proudly called, "Come everyone, see. Here's our banner. Can you boys put it up somehow?"

"Ad Astra Per Aspera," the boys read, recognized the words from the Christmas program.

Hartley read it aloud, and reminded the little ones, "It says 'to the stars through difficulty'; It is Kansas' motto, because that was how we got our star into the flag as a new state. Now it's our school's motto too."

"Sure, we can put it up," Laddie said. "The hedge trees are charred on top, but that's all. We can find a couple of good ones for poles."

While the boys dug holes, the girls tied the banner to the hedge posts by the four corners with twine poked into holes in the sacks. They pounded in some nails to hold against the strong winds. The boys dug holes, set the saplings in and packed them solid.

As the early morning sun struck the banner, which billowed in the breeze, the black charcoal outlines filled with red mulberry stain and edged with blue against the white sugar sacks seemed to glow with life. It proclaimed, "Ad Astra Per Aspera" with a fat, smiling sunflower whose blue stem grew from a pile of black objects and smeared soot.

Gus suddenly started singing, in his undependably deep voice, "Oh, say can you see, by the dawn's early light ..."

All of them, standing at attention, joined in with "What so proudly we hailed ..."

So intent they were that they did not hear the new arrivals until three wagons pulled into the schoolyard. Heinie and Rube Pfitzer were in the first, accompanied by a stranger in a flat, black hat. Four other black-hatted strangers were in the other wagons, and all three wagons were loaded. Tied to the Pfitzer wagon were two dun-colored oxen.

Heinie explained, "This here's Chris Muller, and he brought some friends. They are Mennonites from the settlement over behind Newton. They don't talk English, but they know how to make soddies."

Mr. Muller was a spry little man with a twinkling smile who spoke little English. He had brought not only the needed breaking plow, but a big metal scoop to be pulled by a horse.

With the Pfitzers and Dienstetters to translate, the men quickly took charge. They inspected the nearby areas of

173

unbroken prairie grass and agreed on a suitable area to cut. Mr. Muller hitched his sturdy oxen to the plow, and soon the moldboard of three curved rods was turning over neat strips twelve inches apart. With axes and spades, Pat, Mike, Laddie and three of the newcomer men carefully measured thirty-six-inch-long pieces, cut them, and loaded them into the wagon bed.

Meanwhile the fifth man supervised the other boys in cleaning up the debris from the fire. As the dirt floor of what would be the new building was scraped smooth, the girls and little children, with bundles of wet straw, rubbed it until they got past the soot to clean dirt, even and hard.

As the men used more twine to mark lines between corner posts, the first wagonload of carefully stacked sods pulled up. The man they called Jacob began to fit the first layer, grass side down, lengthwise along the twine-marked wall edge.

Two more strips were fitted lengthwise outside that one, and the children all helped with those, laying one as tight as possible next to the strip already down, and then another beside it.

When they were partway down the long wall, another man, Fritz, began at the first end. He laid sods crossways over the first ones, carefully fitting them to keep the edges even in spite of the dangling charred grass. Often he stood back and squinted along the line of the wall, standing a straight board on the floor and pushing it against the sods, sometimes shifting one to keep the wall straight.

Pat and Mike got annoyed because the men did not let then lay any sods after the first ones.

"After all, didn't we build our own house? We had Father's help, of course, but he didn't know any more about it than we did!"

"And whose schoolhouse is this, anyway?"

But their sisters calmed them.

"The men are giving their time, and they don't know English. They don't understand that you know so terribly much. Soon enough you'll be building your own soddy, like as not, so do as they say and be glad."

"You might even possibly learn a thing or two."

When noon came, they were all glad. The walls were rising like magic, straight and solid, as all four men swung along as a practiced team. When the sun shone straight down, Chris drove in himself with the latest load of sods, and announced, "Now is time we eat."

The children had been carrying sods, hauling up buckets of water for the men to smooth each layer before they put on the next and burying ashes. They were all glad to stop.

The men washed first. By the time the big sisters had scrubbed themselves and the little ones free from most of the soot on their faces and hands and started to get out lunch baskets, the visitors had lifted out of their wagons a variety of hampers and tubs.

"Is feast for everyone," Chris beamed.

He handed a pile of white cloth to Kathleen and asked her to spread it on the ground. From the hampers began to come food and food and more food.

The word quickly passed among the children, "Eat polite like on Fridays."

Polite they were, and eat they did. Some of the food was familiar, but much was new—mixtures of meat and dumplings, meat and noodles, thick bread slices and sweet butter, cake and pie, pickles and jam and preserves.

Hartley confided to Gus, "I don't think I can move again," as he took one more bit of a delicious new sweet stuff Gus said was watermelon preserves.

"Remember Miss Jorgensdatter talking about watermelons in Wichita? These is made from the rinds."

"I'm going to get us some seeds of those. They are as

good as she said to eat, and then you can make stuff like this out of the peelings."

By the end of the meal even the younger children had gotten over their shyness. Tessie whispered to Gus and then said carefully to Fritz, "Danke. Es goot."

Fritz looked surprised, then laughed heartily. Although he answered in his own language, the pat on her head needed no translation.

The children were surprised by the arrival of Mr. Dawson and Mr. Moore in the Dawson buggy, but not so surprised as the fathers were to see the strangers and the half-finished walls. The fathers had come to help the boys start laying sods!

Gus Pfitzer was sent home. He returned with two sacks balanced across his saddle—one of sand, one of clay—from what they kept on hand at home for patching. The girls had already begun to "plaster" the inside, troweling the mixture onto the ends of the sod blocks to make a smooth surface, finishing with a little plain water.

"Someday we will whitewash it all," they planned.

Mr. Dawson had brought some leftover boards that he had carefully saved from the building of his own house. He donated them for the needed supports at the tops of the doors and windows.

The upper part, which had to be done from ladders, was slower. But before the shadows got too long in the west, the call from Jacob, translated by Gus, was that the last line of wall sods was finished. The doorways had sill boards, two pieced upright boards to hold the sides, and a sturdy crosspiece at the top extending into the sods at the sides to support the wall above. The window openings had top boards; bottom and side boards could be fitted in sometime later when windows were added. The big open fireplace was built into the north wall and out a ways into the room. A stove could be fitted into it sometime later.

Mr. Dawson spoke a little German; Chris Muller a little English. Mr. Dienstetter had quit plowing early to come help a little, so the men managed to talk some as they washed and reloaded the visitors' wagons.

"You haf enuf sod cut for de roof, Mr. Dawson. If de poys pile it inside and cover it, some rain might come won't hurt."

"I thank you so much, Mr. Muller. Now, as soon as we can get a ridgepole and maybe some cut branches for support, we can lay the roof ourselves."

Chris interrupted, his eyes twinkling, "I tink you do not vait long for ridgepole—und maybe eefen flat boards and tar paper for under de sod roof."

"Well, we will try as fast as we can. But I am afraid it will be awhile. But if crops are good this year, and grasshoppers don't come back, like last year ..."

Chris laughed. "No, I tink you don't vait for crops for no ridgepole." In German he spoke to the others, who laughed in turn. They all shook hands vigorously with the local men, and with the children.

"Gute Kinder! Brave Kinder!" they said, and began to pull out of the schoolyard, calling, "Gute Nacht!"

As the children and the fathers stood waving good-bye, they discovered two more wagons coming from the south. Everyone wondered who it could be.

Suddenly Phoebe cried, "It's Marietta Stephenson! And her brothers!"

Phoebe ran to meet her friends, who stopped to let her step onto the front hub and then pulled her up to share the front seat. The girls hugged each other, and as the wagon pulled up in front of the new walls, Roger Stephenson read out loud the words on the red, white and blue banner, "'Ad astra per aspera' with a phoenix sunflower! Phoebe, I'll bet you had a hand in that."

"We all helped," Phoebe explained modestly.

"Well, folks, I can see you have been busy," Richard Stephenson shook hands with the men, and they exchanged names.

"We've come to help a little, and brought some stuff you might need."

Mr. Dawson for once was speechless.

Marietta was bubbling with excitement as they all began to inspect the wagonloads.

Richard went on, "You can imagine how surprised we were to read about the children's escape and how proud we were of them! Roger and I were loading some cattle at Newton where we met a friend who had to change his plans because his sod-cutter had a rush job on a schoolhouse. He said the children who got burned out had decided to build a new one for themselves.

"So we hunted up Chris Muller and got more details. Bud, Roger and I and a few friends around who had read about the fire and wanted to help got together some boards for your roof and windows and doors and some tar paper. We got a couple of good straight walnut trees for the ridgepole. Walnut is strong and we can lash them together."

Roger said, "We thought we'd spend the night with you folks, and see if we can't get that roof on tomorrow. Muller said he'd leave enough cut sods."

Marietta was pulling at things in the first wagon.

"And Phoebe, Maureen, Kathleen, Helga—under the seat here. From Mother and some of the neighbor women who heard, there's piles of braided rag rugs and two bushels of torn and sewed carpet rags you can make some more with. The women said they would collect some more and send them as soon as they could so you'll have something to sit on until you get a wood floor and some desks and seats."

The newcomers did most of the talking. The others were numb after so much excitement and so many surprises. But as they all went inside to inspect the plastering, they were surprised again to find a new structure at the far end of the building.

"It's a desk—for the teacher," Sean explained proudly.

The younger children had found little to do in the afternoon, and someone had used broken pieces of sod to build a desk. The busy workers had paid no attention to their play.

"It doesn't have any pull drawers, but see, it's got a piece scooped out for her feet—and this big, smooth top to put books on when we get some. We used the edge of a board to scrape it even, like the men did, and then put on some of the girls' plaster and smoothed it good. And we're going to get a nail keg for a stool, because whoever is teacher should not have to sit on the floor, do you think?"

Friday morning Mr. Dawson said, "Since this is the way the Lord seems to be pointing, the plowing will just have to wait another day."

And with the Stephensons, the Dawsons went back to help with the roof. The word had spread, and a number of other fathers arrived; even some district patrons who were not yet fathers showed up to help. Most surprising, Mr. Lancey, gruff as always and spitting a long distance every little while, came ready to work.

"Pa's funny these days," Bart told Hartley as they unloaded sods. "Ever since Wade turned on him. Wade's going to be all right, the doctor says. I guess Wade and the teacher are going to get married and homestead after harvest. They're talking about her helping him study nights until he can get ready for college. Then he'll farm in the summers enough to prove up his claim and she'll teach school and help him go to college in the winters until he can be a lawyer. Sounds funny, but that's what they say. And Pa—I don't know if he'll ever be hisself again."

"Maybe she can teach our school!"

"I don't reckon. They talked about it. She'd love to, she said, but she better teach in the city where she can get more money. A man going to college, even where it's free, he's got to sleep somewhere and eat even if he ain't working."

This time the Pfitzers brought a whole wagonload of sand and clay and all who were not helping on the roof troweled plaster inside as far up as they could reach. The girls had arranged the rescued pieces of books in rows along the deep window ledges. Tessie laid one open on top of the built-in desk.

"So it will look like a real school."

The ridgepole was placed and the flat boards were laid from it to the walls and a couple of feet beyond to make an overhang. The tar paper was laid over that, then a layer of clay was spread on.

"Sure, I wish we could have put tar paper on ours," Mike exclaimed. "It would keep out the snakes and mice that nest in the roof sod. It would also keep the rain out so Mother and the girls wouldn't have to be holding an umbrella over the fire to cook."

Over the clay came the final layer of sod, grass-side up this time, laid from the ridgepole to the eaves. A few more rounds of sods built up the chimney for a good draft. Except for the window glass and a door, the sod schoolhouse was ready.

The last bit finished, the workers stood about, wiping their hands on their clothes and admiring.

"I can't believe it," Phoebe finally said. "Only a week ago we had the fire and smoke, mud and wind—it seemed like the end of the world. And now! Here is our new schoolhouse!"

"The Phoenix School," Roger said.

"You said that before," Hartley spoke up. "What's a phoenix?"

"Don't you know? The phoenix was as big as an eagle, a beautiful scarlet and gold, and it made a beautiful sound. There was never but one at a time. After it lived five hundred years or so it burned in its nest, and out of the ashes a new phoenix sprang up, more beautiful than ever. They thought it was like the sun, which dies every night but always is born again the next morning."

"That's good! Maybe we should name it Phoenix School instead of Freedom School."

Richard smiled thoughtfully.

"In a way, they are pretty much the same, Hartley. Freedom keeps dying, but it keeps getting reborn. So Freedom School fits just as well."

It was hard to leave, but leave they must. The Stephensons had a long drive, and the rest knew the milking was waiting.

Saturday they all worked hard at home, trying to make up time. But Sunday the parents agreed that the children could take their lunches and "try out" their new school. Mr. and Mrs. Dawson and some other parents had promised to drive over in the afternoon for the mothers to see the "wonder and the glory."

But near dinnertime a buggy drove into the Dawson yard.

"Professor Carroll! What a nice surprise!"

"Mr. Dawson, Mrs. Dawson. I was shocked to read about your fire and so glad to hear the children got out. Are they really all right?"

"A few colds, nothing serious. Wade Lancey, the young man who really saved them, was the only one who was seriously hurt. But the doctor says he will soon be fine."

"Talk about courage! And discipline! Real self-discipline

when it counted! And what have you thought of our Miss Jorgensdatter?"

The Dawsons laughed.

"Different people think different things, but all of them good," Mr. Dawson summed up. "We certainly can't thank you enough for her. Someday I only hope you can find us another half as great—when we are ready."

"That was really what I came for, Mr. Dawson," Professor Carroll said as he accepted the invitation to have dinner with them, and all were settled.

"A Mr. Sheldon Gould from Massachusetts wrote me— a long night letter by wire, actually—seems he had heard of me from the children when he was here. He has written to you, but he knew it would take time for a letter.

"He wants you to know that friends Back East are sorry about the fire and proud of the children for being splendid young Americans. They don't want children like that to be cheated out of a chance for school. So Mr. Gould and his friends are getting up a subscription to help build a new schoolhouse; they thought you should know as soon as possible, while you were trying to make decisions. They don't know how much money, but Gould said, 'Tell him we will see there is enough!' They don't know just how much such a building will cost to replace out here."

Professor Carroll had his turn at surprise then, as Mr. Dawson told him all that had happened.

"But we are grateful beyond words for their interest, Professor Carroll. And I am wondering—since we don't really need the money for a building—do you suppose Mr. Gould and his friends would be just as willing to have us use the money to pay a schoolteacher?

"You see," he explained, "we made a mistake at first; we put our money into a building and thought we could skimp paying a teacher. We learned better."

Professor Carroll laughed.

"That is strange. I have just come from a visit with John Blevens, the Butler County superintendent. He says that the big trouble with the schools is the prevalent idea among patrons that everyone can teach school."

"Our patrons will tell you, professor, that is not so. We learned the hard way. Our first teacher was an ignorant bully who did much harm and little good. Mr. Gould was an inspiration, but he himself said there was too much he did not know about managing children of all ages and teaching them what each one needed.

"Then your Miss Jorgensdatter took over, and we all learned what a teacher could do who knew the skills of her profession and was herself an educated, cultivated person.

"Even before the fire we were wondering if there was any way we could manage to keep her another year. Our trouble is she is going to get married to her star trouble-maker, Wade Lancey, the hero of the fire."

"No!"

"Seems she decided it would take a lifetime to civilize him, and Wade thinks so, too. They are making plans to homestead and then get him ready to come to you, and finally to be a lawyer. That takes money. We raised our salary to twenty-five dollars a month to get her, but she can make more in the city."

"I see!"

"I think she wants to stay as much as we want her. If we could use some of the subscription money to supplement what we can pay, and if crops are good and the district continues to grow, in another year or two we could possibly raise enough for a good salary on our own."

"Mr. Dawson, I have always thought a country schoolteacher should get more than one in the city—they have so much more responsibility. I am sure Mr. Gould and his friends will be glad to have you use the money the way you think best," Professor Carroll said.

"Wouldn't you like to drive over with us and see the building and the children? I suspect quite a few of them will have turned up. You can give them the news about Mr. Gould. They will be glad to see you."

"I would not miss it for anything!"

The new schoolhouse, with its brown sides and grass roof, did not show up sharply on the horizon as the white frame building had. They were almost upon it before Professor Carroll realized what he was looking at.

In fact, what he saw first was the white banner, billowing gently. When they had stopped, he sat for a few minutes, reading the words under his breath. He bit his lip and looked at Mr. Dawson. Saying nothing, he simply shook his head.

The three baby girls were taking naps in the buggy. The grownups went over to inspect. They paused beside the open doorway, as they heard a general groan come from inside. Then Phoebe's voice said, "Sorry, Kurt. There's two l's in 'parallel' in the middle. Hartley, please spell separate."

Hartley's voice spelled confidently, "s-e-p-e—" only to be interrupted by another groan.

"Both sides even!" Gopher announced.

Just then Phoebe saw the newcomers in the doorway. She was flustered to see Professor Carroll, but thinking of how Miss Jorgensdatter would act, she took a deep breath and smiled.

"Good afternoon, Professor Carroll. Please come in. We are sorry we cannot offer you a chair."

Excitedly, they all looked and laughed.

"Go on—don't let us interrupt you," her father urged.

"We were ready to stop. This is a good place; both sides won! Maybe Professor Carroll would be willing to say a few words."

"I think he would. In fact, he has some wonderful news for you."

Professor Carroll was greeted with loud hand clapping. Phoebe took a place among the lined-up scholars between Kathleen and Helga Dienstetter. Both of them nudged her with their elbows and grinned at her, and Maureen whispered, "Why didn't you tell us he was coming!"

But soon Professor Carroll's news had them all at attention. When they understood that his news meant that they probably could have Miss Jorgensdatter back, they exploded into yells. Dancing and pounding each other, they created general chaos.

When they had quieted, Professor Carroll added, "I just want to say, my young friends, I am terribly proud of all of you. And I envy you. I only wish I could have gone to a school like yours."

David spoke up, "You can come to ours. Everyone is welcome."

The older ones laughed. Hartley tried to shush David, but Professor Carroll thanked him and said, "I wish I could. I am sure I would learn a great deal."

Gus asked, "Before we go, could we hear Gopher's natural history report? He didn't get to give it because of the fire, and he worked awfully hard on it. It's not long."

"Of course! Of course!"

The grownups settled themselves against the walls, the children sat on the floor, and Gopher, looking nervously over his shoulder, was half pushed by Hartley and Sean into the center of the room.

He had not counted on such an audience, but he had practiced hard, and once he got started he sailed through.

He held up a wheat seed and began to read his report entitled "Seeds":

"Folks, this here is a wheat seed like you all know. You can't hardly see it, probably, it is so little. I am going to tell you about mustard seeds. They are so little it would take a lot of them to make one wheat seed. But they got lots of power. Some of them ground up makes a plaster to put on your chest for pneumonia. Just one seed grows to a bush ten, fifteen feet tall. Just a few mustard greens makes a whole pot of beans taste better. Jesus said if anybody's got faith as big as one of those teeny mustard seeds, he can move a whole mountain. That, of course, is if he plants the seed in good ground, like Jesus said, and gives it all the encouragement he can so it will have a chance to grow clear up the way it was meant to. That's all, folks."

The End